AF229473

# The Promised Journey

## Book One of Etta's Story

ISBN 978-1-5323-8863-7

Published by Cherie Coon

Cover design by
SelfPubBookCovers.com/ SandfordCovers

# Books By Cherie Coon

Saga of Yani Series
Yani and the Knapper   the Journey Begins
Yani and the Seapeople   Taken
Yani and Etta   a New Beginning

Etta's Story Series
The Promised Journey

# Part One

# In the Valley

# Chapter One

Etta shaded her eyes from the morning sun as she crossed the village on her way to the beach. She had slipped out early while everyone else was still sleeping so she could enjoy the morning quiet. The air was still cool and crisp with touches of frost in the shaded areas. Savoring the peace of the early morning, she had nearly made it to where the trail left the Valley on its way along the river to the sea when she heard a small voice call her name.

"Etta, wait for me! I want to come, too. I can help you!" called Cru as he ran to catch up.

"What are doing up so early, Cru?" asked Etta. "You're usually the last one to appear in the morning."

"I was sleeping then I saw you walking across the Valley and I knew you would need me to help you. What do you need me to help you with anyway?" asked the skinny little boy.

Etta pushed the boy's rust colored hair out of his eyes and asked, "And just how did you see me leaving if you were sleeping?"

Cru's face took on a puzzled look. He scratched his head and rubbed one barefoot through the dirt, then looked up at Etta with a bright smile. "I was sleeping with my eyes open."

Laughing, Etta said, "Okay, you can come with me but first you need to run back and let someone know you are with me so no one will worry about you."

Nodding he turned back toward the village and started to run. He had only gone a few steps when he stopped and turned back toward Etta. "You will wait for me, won't you?"

"I will wait," assured Etta. "Now go."

As Cru ran back to tell his mother that he was going with Etta, she sat down on the large boulder that marked the entry to the riverside trail. While she waited, she watched the river running high on its way to the sea. The winter had been a long one with more snow than usual. When spring had finally come the people of the Valley were running low on food. For the last moon they had had little to eat but the jerked venison they had made last fall. The village had done their best to prepare for winter -drying berries and vegetables, smoking fish, jerking venison- but the snow came early ending most of the hunting and had continued to fall every few days all winter. Luckily just before the snows set in, the hunters had been unusually successful and had killed not only several deer but two elk as well. Had they not had the extra meat they would have known starvation before spring. Now that the snow had melted, the villagers were all busy foraging for what food they could find to add to their diet. The spring greens had just started to appear in the meadow and after the winter of dried and salted food, they were a special treat.

"Etta!" Cru's cry broke Etta musing. "Mother said I could go with you. She told me to be good and mind you. Why does she always tell me that do you suppose?"

"Maybe because you have a problem remembering to do just that," laughed Etta. "Come on. We need to hurry or the tide will be coming in before we get there."

When they reached the shore, Etta moved along the edge of the water looking for a likely rock. After checking several, she found one that was covered with hundreds of black mussels. She took off her moccasins, careful to put them above the high-water mark. Setting her basket just out of reach of the waves, she waded into the shallow water.

"Is the water cold?" asked Cru.

"What do you think?" asked Etta. "Why don't you come in with me and see for yourself?"

The boy inched forward cautiously until the water lapped against his toes. With a squeal he jumped back. Etta laughed, then said, "Why don't you stay where you are. It is really cold. It won't take me long to pry loose enough mussels for a nice stew for supper tonight."

"Will you tell me a story while you work?" asked Cru.

"What kind of story do you want?" asked Etta as she pried another mussel from the rock with her flint knife.

"I don't care. Any story you like."

"All right. How about this. See this mussel?" she said holding up one of the shells. "Inside it is the first part of my life. In the beginning I lived in the Village in the Marsh with my mother and father. Our village was on a small island in the middle of a shallow marsh. To catch fish, we only had to walk to the edge of the marsh and throw in our line. And ducks came every spring and fall to rest on their journeys. Not all of them continued their trips north and south though. Some of them made their way into our stomachs," laughed Etta, as she tossed another mussel into the basket. "Those were the ducks I liked the best."

"If you lived on an island, how did you get to it in the winter? Did you use a boat like the Seapeople?" asked the boy.

"A Seapeople's boat would be way too big for the marsh. No, we just walked on water to get to the village." Etta tossed a few more mussels in the basket as she grinned at Cru.

"No. You're kidding me. No one can walk on water," cried Cru. "That's just silly."

"Oh, but it's true, Cru," she said as she threw another handful of mussels into the basket. "At least it appeared that you were walking on water. There was a secret causeway that you walked over to get to the island in the middle. They had built it up with rocks and clay then topped it with steppingstones. It was a zig zag path so you had to know the way or you would step off into the water."

"Oh, that sounds like fun," said Cru.

"You wouldn't think so if you saw the water. It was always brown and murky."

"Yuck," said Cru. "You're right. I wouldn't like to swim there."

"Now, this mussel holds the second part of my life," continued Etta showing the shell to Cru. "The fire. I know you have heard the adults talk about it but I remember it through a child's eyes. The men had all gone to a faraway river to catch salmon. The women had gone off to look for berries and nuts. It had been a long hot summer and everything was really dry. Fin and I had stayed in the village with Loki and Lamu. Lamu had a cold and Loki stayed to look after us all. I was about the same age as you. How many summers are you, Cru?"

"I'm six summers now. Or will be when it's summer."

"Then yes I was just your age. Fin was one summer more. We were playing a game with Lamu outside her house when Fin noticed the smoke. Lamu looked up and saw the fire coming. We grabbed sleeping cloaks to cover with and ran to the causeway. We spent a scary night in the water as the fire burned all around us. Do you remember Loki?"

"Yes, she was Dan's grandmother and she had scars all over her back."

"That's right. She was burned during the fire. The wind blew part of a burning roof on to her as she tried to get back to the causeway. She had gone to check on the old grandmothers who lived on the other side of the island. But she was too late. The grandmothers had been caught by the fire. Loki had almost made it to the causeway when the burning thatch landed on her. Lamu had to go kick it off her. It was so scary. After the fire, the men who survived came home and we went to Yani's beach. None of the women and only three of the men came home. My mother and father were not among them."

Etta was silent for a while as she pried several more mussels off the rock. Cru waited patiently then whispered. "What happened next?"

"Well, this mussel is our life in the Valley. You were too little to remember the trip here after the fire. You were just a baby.

I just remember being tired from all the walking. But once we got here and got our houses built it was a good place to live."

Etta threw a last handful of mussels in the basket and said, "My feet are frozen. I need to warm them up a bit. And this is enough mussels anyway. Let me cover this with seaweed then we can look for some crabs while the tide is still out."

Etta scooped a big handful of seaweed from the water's edge then laid it over the mussels in the basket. When she had the top covered, she carried the basket up the beach above the high-water mark where she had left her moccasins. The sun-warmed sand felt good on Etta's cold feet as they walked along the edge of the water. At each tide pool they stopped and looked for the hard-shelled creatures with the sharp claws that they had discovered were a tasty addition to their diet. It was early in the year to be finding them but still it was worth the time to look. When the pools had all been swallowed up by the rising tide, they gave up. Empty handed they walked back to where they had left the basket of mussels.

After brushing the sand from her feet, Etta pulled on her moccasins. With the basket resting on her hip, she took Cru's hand and they started up the path to the Valley. They had only gone a short distance when Cru asked, "Do you miss your mother and father?"

Etta was silent for a moment. She fingered the stone that hung from the cord around her neck. It had been her father's. Sighing deeply, she replied, "In the beginning I did. You know, Fin lost his parents, too. We both hoped they would come back at first. I remember one day while we were camped on the beach on our way to the Valley, Fin was explaining to me that our parents weren't coming back. Since he's one summer older than I am he understood more. At your age one summer makes an enormous difference. Anyway, Yani overheard us talking. I'm sure there was a lot of fear in our voices so she came over to comfort us. She told us that we would always have a family in the Valley. We could choose where we wanted to live when we got settled. Or we could move from house to house. As you know I chose to live with Yani. Fin drifted about at the start but finally settled down with Birg and Ami. I think he chose them because he likes the goats so much."

"What do you think your next mussel will be?" asked the boy when Etta had finished.

Etta laughed looking down at the boy. "Who knows?" she said. "Maybe when Deet heads out this winter on his trading journey, I'll go with him. A long time ago he promised me when I was twelve summers I could. Maybe Yani, Deet and I will go all the way to the Mountains That Are Always White. Yani has said she would like to visit her mother's village one more time."

"Can I come, too?" asked Cru eagerly.

"I don't think so. At least not this year. It is an awfully long dangerous journey. Maybe when you are twelve summers you will get the chance."

# Chapter Two

Yani was stirring up the embers in the firepit when Etta and Cru came down the three steps into her house. Yani's house had been built in the manner of the Seapeople, partly underground, keeping it cooler in the summer and warmer in the winter. She had learned about this type of house when she had lived for a year with the Seapeople across the sea to the north. Deet was on the sleeping bench at the back fastening a new blade to the head of his spear. A large wolf with a gray muzzle lay at the man's feet. The wolf raised his head when Etta and Cru entered but once he saw who it was, he returned to his nap.

"It looks like you two have been to the beach," said Yani. "And it looks like we will be having mussels tonight. My mouth is watering just thinking about it. It's been ages since we had any. Thank you, Etta."

"We looked for crabs too but didn't find any," said Cru. "I like them better than mussels. But I like mussels too. I can eat with you, can't I?" added Cru. "I helped Etta."

Etta looked at him with raised eyebrows.

"Well, I talked to her when she was gathering them so that is kind of helping," added Cru.

"Of course, you can eat with us" said Yani with a smile. "But first you need to tell your mother where you are."

"Okay," replied Cru as he hesitated at the door. "You won't eat them all before I get back, will you?'"

"Better hurry then because I'm about to starve and I love mussels," called Deet from his spot in the back of the house. "Matter of fact that looks just about the right amount for me."

"I'll hurry," called Cru as he turned toward the door. "Don't let him eat them all, Yani."

"It's all right Cru. We aren't going to eat them until later. But you can come back once you tell Dami where you are. Maybe you can talk Deet into telling you a story."

"Oh boy, a story!" he cried as he ran up the steps and out the door.

"That boy has more energy that any child I have ever met," said Yani shaking her head. "You better start thinking of a story for him, Deet."

"Maybe it's not that he has so much energy but that we're slowing down, my sweet butterfly dancer," said Deet. "It has been many summers since I have seen you frolicking with a cloud of butterflies."

"Oh, Deet, I did that when I was a child," replied Yani with a sigh.

Etta wasn't sure if she should slip out and let them remember their past alone or interrupt them. In the end she chose to slip out. Grabbing a large clay pot streaked with soot from the fire she ducked out the door. The wolf followed behind her as she left the house. Patting the wolf's head, she turned toward the spring that trickled down out of the cliff sheltering the Valley. The cliff was honeycombed with shallow caves. They had lived in one of them their first winter here until they could get their houses built. They still used some of the caves to house the sheep and goats in the winter. They also used them to store the hay to feed the animals.

When they reached the spring, Etta set the pot under the trickle of water to fill, then sat down on a rock. "Come here, Wolf,": said Etta. "You are getting old too, aren't you?" The large animal laid his massive head on Etta's knee. She scratched behind his ears and patted his big head. They sat there for a while watching the village going about its business in the Valley below. Ami and Dan were walking hand in hand to the goat pen with a basket of old pumpkins to feed to them. Dan was chattering to her but they were too far away for Etta to hear what they were saying. Dorf, Sven, and Fin were heading into the forest to the west of the Valley to hunt. She loved the peace of the Valley.

"Got you!" yelled Cru as he jumped at her from behind a nearby boulder. As soon as he landed Wolf leaped at him knocking him off his feet. Cru squealed as the wolf held him down and licked his face.

"I'd say it looks like Wolf got you," said Etta with a chuckle. "What's that all over you face? Wolf seems to like it."

Pushing Wolf away Cru managed to get to his feet. "Mother was at Honi's house when I found her. She and Honi had been picking dandelion greens. Boy, did they have a lot of them. I don't like them because they are so bitter but Yani says I need to eat them, so I can grow up big and strong. So, I guess I will eat them."

"Cru, your face?" prompted Etta.

"What about my face?" asked Cru.

"I asked you what you had all over your face?"

"Oh, that. Well, when I told Mother that I was going to eat mussels with Yani she said I still had to eat breakfast. I tried to talk her out of it. But Honi made me eat some acorn porridge before she let me go. I guess I got it all over my face. I'm still not sure why I had to eat porridge when I'm going to eat mussels.""

"She was wise. The mussels won't be ready until later. We're having them for supper," said Etta.

"Oh," said the boy. "Then I guess it is good that Mother made me eat."

"I guess it was," said Etta. "Come on. The water jug is full. Let's take it back to Yani."

# Chapter Three

That evening after they had eaten the last of the mussels the talk turned to the plans for the summer. Everyone in the Valley shared the work of the village. Yani and Etta oversaw the garden and herb gathering. Honi, Dami, and Lamu were in charge of baking the bread. The men did the hunting. Ami with the help of the young children took care of the goats and sheep. Deet and Birg were the traders. All in all, summer was a busy time.

"I've been thinking of starting an herb garden," said Etta. "If I work up a patch at the edge of the woods near where the path enters it, I think I can get the herbs we use the most to grow there. We'll still have to gather some of them but this will reduce the distance you have to walk," she said to Yani.

"Are you saying I'm getting too old to go out and gather," asked Yani.

"No, I know you can still walk all the way to the Mountains That Are Always White if you have a mind to. But wouldn't it be nice not to have to walk quite so much?"

"As always you're right," replied Yani. "But I'll still walk as often as possible. If I don't, I'll forget how."

"If you forget how, I'll teach you again," said Cru, as he reached out and patted the old woman's hand.

"And I'm sure you'll do a marvelous job of it too. I will keep that in mind."

"How about you, Deet? Do you have any big plans for this summer and next winter's trading journey?" asked Etta.

"I'll probably help Birg make salt. That seems to be the best trade item besides Yani's blades. And as to your blades," he said to Yani. " I have to come up with a story to explain them. I can't keep telling them the Knapper made them but is too old to travel. He was too old to travel when you came to live with him. I can't tell them that the girl who used to live with him makes them so I have to have a different story."

'I can see that's a problem. Not too many men will accept that the blades they're using are made by a woman. I guess you could tell them that they were made by a young man Knut taught before he passed to the Otherside," said Yani.

"Or you could just say they were made by his student. You don't have to say his student is a woman," suggested Etta.

"I guess that would work but why is the student not trading the blades himself?" asked Deet?

"You could say that a bear bit his legs off," said Cru. "He couldn't walk if that happened. Dan said if I'm not careful about wandering off into the woods that's what's going to happen to me."

"Now that is a very good idea," replied Yani stifling a laugh. "But maybe just say he fell and broke his leg badly and it didn't heal right. After all something like that happened to the Knapper. He was lucky that he could still walk even if it was with a limp. I think that has to be your story. Before he died, the Knapper took on a crippled boy and taught him much like the Knapper learned his trade."

"Why did the Knapper teach you, Yani, instead of some boy? I know I have to be careful who I tell that you are the knapper for our village," said Cru.

At that, Deet roared with laughter. "He didn't have a choice, Cru. This contrary girl sneaked off and taught herself. When he saw how good she was he had no choice but to finish her training. In no time she was making better blades than he was."

"Now, Deet, I wouldn't say I was better, I just made them a little different," said Yani.

"Will you teach me some time, Yani?' asked Cru.

"Maybe," she replied. "But you need to learn patience first. I'll tell you what. Next time Etta and I make the trip to my old home to gather flint you can come along. Gathering the flint is the first step."

"Oh, boy! Wait until I tell Dan," Cru started saying then paused and thought. "But then he will want to come too. Maybe I should just keep it a secret. But what if he really wants to go too," the boy sputtered to a stop and looked at Yani puzzled.

"I think keeping it a secret for now is just fine. But I'm guessing Dan wouldn't be all that interested in making that long walk. Remember we'll be walking for two days just to get there," said Etta.

"I can do that. I can probably run for two days," said Cru.

"I think you probably can but we can't so let's plan to walk," said Etta. "And now it's time for you to head home. It's past your bedtime. Come on, I'll walk you home."

As they left the house, Yani turned to Deet. "I think it's a good idea to start teaching someone. Cru might just be the right one. If I can get him to stay put long enough."

"If it's something he's interested in he can stay at it for a very long time. Just the other day I watched him as he tried to build a rock tower. I'm not sure why he was building it but he stuck with it for most of the morning. I was scraping that deer skin I had stretched early last the winter. I could see him from where I was working. He would get his tower up to his knees then it would fall over. He would start over changing the way he piled it up. He was still working on it when I finished up the scraping, had rolled up the hide and taken it up to the storage cave. I had worked on it most of the day."

"Then I may be able to teach him. He's a little too young but I can start with the basics. It's too bad Etta didn't want to learn. She would have made a fine knapper," said Yani.

"You know I did try but I just don't have the patience!" said Etta as she entered the house.

"Yes, I know. Maybe I should have tried to teach Fin,"

"It's not too late to teach him. He is only twelve summers," said Deet.

"Well, maybe," replied Yani. "But now it's time to sleep.

# Chapter Four

Etta loved the feeling of the warm sun on her back as she worked up a patch of earth for her herb garden. She had chosen a spot near the woods that would be shaded part of the day when the heat of summer finally arrived. Now the path the sun took across the sky was still low enough on the horizon that it hit the patch only a brief time each day. But it was enough to melt the frozen ground making it possible to dig it up. Later in the season when the sun had risen higher in the sky the area would get more sun. Not enough to bake the woodland plants she hoped to make grow here but enough for them to grow strong and healthy. She didn't say it again to Yani but she knew it would be a help to her. Wandering the woods and meadows in search of the medicine plants she needed was taking more and more of a toll on her. Etta had seen a big change in her just since last summer.

As she worked Cru wandered by. "Can I help, Etta?" he asked.

"You can gather up the rocks and pile them over there," she said pointing to a pile of rocks she had already moved out of the worked area. "And you can break up the clumps of dirt, too."

As Etta dug into the dirt with her stone hoe, he began picking up the big clumps of soil and breaking them apart. They worked quietly for a while when Cru asked, "Do you think I can learn to be a knapper? Yani said she would try to teach me."

"I don't know why not. If you work at it, that is."

"But you couldn't learn so it must be hard," replied Cru.

"It isn't easy, I admit but I did get to the point I could make a decent blade. I just didn't like doing it," said Etta. "You know it means you have to sit still for a long time at a stretch. You've watched Yani. Sometimes she'll work at it for the whole day."

"I guess I need to practice doing something for a long time. Like helping you. I'll help you all day. That will mean I can do it, right?"

"I don't know about that, but it's a start."

The sun was low in the west and the air had taken on a chill when Etta and Cru finally finished the new garden patch. Etta was pleasantly surprised that Cru had stuck with it for so long. He was usually such a gadfly. As they walked together back toward the village, they detoured past the spring to wash the dirt from their hands and face. The cool water felt good after the hard work.

As they entered the house, Yani said, "There you are Cru. I was wondering where you were off to. I thought you were going to watch me make blades today."

"I forgot," cried Cru. "I was helping Etta. I'm sorry."

"And he was a very good helper. He worked with me all afternoon and didn't wander off once," said Etta.

"Does this mean you aren't going to teach me?" asked Cru. "I promise to remember the next time."

"Never mind, Cru," replied Yani. "There's plenty of time. But you better go let your mother know where you are. She has been looking for you."

As soon as the boy left, Etta joined Yani by the firepit to help prepare the evening meal. Yani already had a pot of water warming on the fire. As it came to a boil, she chopped the fresh green stems of wild onions that grew near the river and added them to the hot water. She also had a handful of young dandelion leaves that she had found in the meadow. They were still small but soon the meadow would be full of the bitter green plants that perked everyone up after a winter of dried food.

When the water came back to a boil, she added some acorn meal which was the staple of their diet. After stirring it into the water she added some small pieces of jerky. It was the last of the dried venison from the deer Deet had killed the previous fall. With luck the hunters would be bringing fresh meat soon.

As the meal cooked, Yani said, "I think we should make that trip to my old home for flint sometime soon. It won't be long until it's time to start planting. I won't want to take time away from the gardens to make the trip then. You have the herb garden ready for the plants when they start coming up. I know they won't be coming up in the woods for a while yet. So, I think now is the best time."

"I'll be ready whenever you are," replied Etta. "I think we should take Cru. I'm fairly sure he can make the trip.+

"I have no doubt he can make the trip. I've never seen anyone with more energy," replied Yani with a laugh.

Three days later, as the sun was peeking over the horizon far out to sea, Yani, Etta, Cru and Wolf followed by two of the pack goats started on their journey. Yani had debated whether to bring Wolf's traveling pack to carry the flint nodules home. In the end she decided to use two of the goats that Birg and Deet had trained to carry their trade goods. In all her early travels with the Knapper, Wolf had carried most of their trade items as they made their way from the Mountains That Are Always White and back to their home by the North Sea. Toward the end he had even carried the Knapper when his strength gave out on what was their last trip together. Deet had helped her make the traveling pack from two long poles with vines laced between them. She had used it to transport many things over the years but now Wolf was getting old too. He no longer could carry the loads of his youth. But the goats would do fine. They carried heavy loads when Deet and Birg made their trading journeys over the winter. They would be able to carry enough nodules to keep her busy for a long time. She realized that she too was getting old. The trip to her beach became harder each time.

By night fall they had made it to the stream that trickled out of the dunes before running across the beach into the sea. They had camped and rested here on the trek from Yani's beach to the Valley after the fire. They had survived the fire but they had lost their homes. In the end it turned out that the Valley provided an ideal place for them. But they didn't know that when they sadly left their home near the beach.

They made a cold supper of jerky and were soon sound asleep. During the night Yani was awakened by Wolf's soft growl. As she listened for what had awakened him, she heard the warbling call of the wolf pack hunting in the distance. "You still hear their call, don't you; old friend," she said as she scratched behind his ears. "All these years and the urge to return to the wild is still there." Wolf whined softly before laying his head against Yani's side and settling back to sleep.

Wolf had joined Yani and the Knapper on their first journey south. After following them for days, one snowy night he had walked into the cave they were sheltering in, circled three times, and snuggled down beside Yani. She had only been a young girl of eleven summers when Wolf made them his pack. He has been her companion ever since.

The rising sun woke them the next morning and as soon as they had the packs on the goats, they continued their trek. As the sun was fading, they neared the beach that had been Yani's home until the fire devastated the forest on the top of the cliff. She had managed to save some of her belongings because, as luck would have it, she had been bringing a load of reeds from the dunes. She had the traveling pack attached to Wolf loaded with the reed. They had just reached her house at the top of the cliff when she saw the smoke from the fire. She was able to throw the reeds off and fill it with as much as possible before sending Wolf back to the beach. Then she filled a large basket and followed him. The others from the meadow were not able to save as much but between them they had enough to survive the first winter in the Valley.

As they neared Yani's beach, Wolf began to softly growl. He was using his "there is danger ahead" growl. The group stopped. Yani whispered to Etta, "Take Cru and the goats into the dunes and keep them there. Stay silent. If anything happens to me take Cru and go home. Do you understand me?"

Etta nodded. Yani looked sternly at Cru until he too nodded.

As soon as Etta, Cru and the goats had slipped away, Yani and Wolf eased their way on up the beach. They had almost reached her beach when the wind shifted and she heard the sound of voices. They dropped down behind one of the large rocks that were scattered along the beach and watched. It wasn't long before three strange men emerged from the trail up the cliff and walked out onto the beach. As soon as she saw them, she pulled her sling from the belt at her waist. Looking through the rocks at her feet she chose several well shaped pebbles and placed them on the big rock within easy reach. As Yani watched, the men moved along the beach picking up rocks and either discarding them or putting them in the pouches they carried. It didn't take Yani long to realize they were here to gather the flint. But whether they were knappers or just here to gather the raw material, she couldn't tell.

She watched until the sun slipped over the cliff in the west then crept back down the beach to where she had left Cru and Etta. As she neared the dunes where she had left them Etta rose up to greet her.

"We're going to have to wait at least a day before we go on. There are three strange men on the beach and I would rather we not be seen. It's probably alright but I had a very odd feeling about them. And Wolf never calmed down the whole time we watched. His ruff on the back of his neck was standing straight up. I think we'll stay here and wait until they leave."

"And, if they don't leave?" asked Etta.

"Then I'll make another plan," replied Yani.

# Chapter Five

It was two days before the strangers on Yani's beach finally left. Each day, Yani and Wolf had crept to the rock where they kept watch. While they were gone Etta and Cru remained in the dunes with the goats. As they waited Etta taught Cru how to weave small baskets from the reeds. By the end of the second day, she knew they would either have to confront the strangers or go back to the stream since they were running low on water. Shortly after the sun had passed its highest point, Yani called to them. As they emerged from the dunes she smiled and said, "They have finally gone. They left just after I got to my lookout point but I waited until I was sure they were gone. Come on let's go gather our flint so we can leave tomorrow at first light."

They moved quickly up the shore to Yani's beach and Etta immediately began looking for the flint Yani needed to make her blades. Yani took Cru's hand and began moving along the rock-strewn beach looking for the right kind of rock. When she found a likely one, she picked it up and showed it to Cru.

"Here is what we are looking for. See how the color is the same throughout? And look at the shape. It is flatter on one end. That's not necessary but it makes it much easier to knap. Now see if you can find one?"

Cru moved off up the beach picking up rocks, then rejecting them, until he finally was satisfied with one. He brought the rock to Yani for her approval. She looked it over carefully then said, "That's just what I need. Now go see if you can find some more."

Etta, Yani and Cru searched the beach for flint until the light began to fade. By that time, they had the goat's pack baskets nearly full. As Yani made a small fire to cook some acorn meal mush for supper, Etta filled the drinking gourds for the next day. The spring that trickled down the cliff near where Yani's cave shelter had once been, was still cold and sweet. Meanwhile Cru was exploring the beach. It didn't take him long to find the shallow cave

Birg had dug into the soft chalk cliff to store his fishing nets and salt making gear.

At first, he was hesitant to enter the cave but finally curiosity got the better of him. After the bright sunshine it took a minute for his eyes to adjust. Wolf had followed him and coming up behind the boy began to growl softly. Cru stopped and looked down at Wolf. "What is it, Wolf?" he asked. "Is there something in there?"

Wolf crept forward then paused, looking back at the boy. Cru moved forward until he was next to Wolf. That's when he heard it. The sound of the waves had drowned out the noise until they were further into the cave. Now he heard a soft mewling sound. As his eyes adjusted more the boy saw a large shape at the back of the cave. It did not seem to be moving but two small objects beside it were. Wolf moved forward and sniffed the air. Then his growl changed tone to a welcoming sound. The two small objects moved forward and Cru saw they were two small animals. Kneeling he reached out a hand to the nearest one. To his surprise sharp tiny teeth nipped his hand.

"Ouch!" cried Cru. "Now, why did you do that. I'm not going to hurt you."

Now that the small creature had moved into the light near the mouth of the cave, Cru saw that it was a baby wolf. Wolf was nudging a full-grown wolf but getting no response. Cru reached out and touched it. He knew at once it was dead. The two small wolves growled with as much fierceness as they could manage when Cru touched their mother.

"Wolf, what should we do with these two babies?" asked Cru. "We can't just leave them here."

As if understanding, Wolf picked one of the pups up by the scruff of his neck and turned toward the opening. As he left the cave the other pup stumbled after him. Cru gave one last look at the dead wolf and followed. As he emerged from the cave, Cru called to Yani. "Yani! Come see what Wolf and I have found."

"In a minute, Cru," replied Yani. "I'm trying to get this fire going so I can cook you some supper."

"But at least look up," cried an exasperated Cru.

"What have you…" Yani looked up to see Wolf walking toward her with the pup in his mouth. Cru was urging the other pup to follow.

"See! I knew you would want to see," said Cru.

"Where on earth did you get those?" asked Etta. "And where's the mother? She won't be happy to see her babies being carried off."

"She's dead," said Cru quietly. "She's in the cave. I think the men who were here when we came killed her."

"Etta, go take a look. Wolf, bring that baby to me," said Yani.

As Etta walked off toward the cave, Wolf laid the pup at Yani's feet. The second pup scrambled over to join its brother. Yani knelt and rubbed her hand over Wolf's back several times. Then she held her hand out to the first of the pups. It sniffed it cautiously. She let it investigate for a while then gently touched its head. It jerked back then stopped. Yani repeated this several times until the pup let her gently pick it up. She petted and nuzzled it a few times then set it back on the beach. Having made peace with the first pup she turned to the second. By this time, Etta had returned and was watching. As Yani gentled the second pup, Etta began the same actions with the first one. Since the pup had been through this with Yani it took only a short time to allow Etta to pick it up. Etta motioned Cru over and handed the pup to him. He very gently petted the small animal and crooned to it softly. Soon he had both pups cuddled in his arms while Etta and Yani returned to preparation for the night.

As they worked Etta talked softly to Yani, "Cru was right. Someone has killed the mother. It looks like not too long ago so he is probably right that it was the men we saw when we arrived. I'm surprised they didn't kill the pups too. And the puzzling thing is they didn't take the pelt."

"That is odd. I'm not sure why they would do that. The only thing I can think is they didn't have sharp enough knives to do it? Maybe that's why they were here gathering flint. I didn't feel comfortable when I saw them. I usually have no fear of strangers but these men were different."

"But why would they need to make their own blades? Everyone knows they can trade for blades in our Valley?" asked Etta.

"Maybe they are outcasts. I couldn't see their faces well enough to see if they had been marked," continued Yani. After a short pause, she continued, "the moon will be full tonight. The sky is clear. I think we should eat, feed these pups, and then start back. I would like to get as far from here tonight as we can."

As they ate, Yani soaked several pieces of jerky in hot water to soften it. She had torn it into little pieces so it would be easier for the pups to eat. Once it had softened, she and Cru coaxed the pups to eat it while Etta caught the goats and loaded them. As the moon rose over the sea, they started the journey back to the Valley.

# Chapter Six

They had covered the fire with sand and roughed up their footprints in the area around it. Luckily, most of the beach was rocky so there was very little evidence of their passing. As soon as they could they started off down the beach.

"Walk in the damp sand below the high tide mark," said Yani as they started down the shore. "I don't want to leave footprints for them to follow."

They walked until the moon was high in the sky and starting the slide down toward the west. By then Cru and the pups were beginning to lag behind. Finally, Cru plopped down on the sand and cried, "I can't walk another step! I need to sleep!" With that he curled up and before Yani and Etta could make camp for the night he was sound asleep. Taking his sleeping cloak, Etta wrapped the boy against the chill of the night.

The sun was well above the horizon when the three travelers woke. The goats had wandered over to the dunes and were grazing on the young sea grass that grew there. Wolf was alert but not in the way that meant there was danger. Yani woke Cru as Etta loaded the goats.

"Come on, Cru, time to wake up. I know you didn't get enough sleep but we will stop earlier tonight." Yani said as she gently shook the boy awake.

He sat up and rubbed his eyes. Looking around he mumbled, "Where am I?"

Yani laughed before tousling his hair. "You're on the first step to becoming a knapper. Remember?"

"Oh, right. We walked all night last night, didn't we," he replied. Scrambling to his feet he started down the beach before he stopped and looked around confused. Yani handed him a piece of jerky and said, "You can chew on this as we walk."

They walked until they reached the stream that had been their first camp site on the trek to Yani's beach. They stopped for a rest and to fill their water gourds then continued on their way. Off and on one of them had to scoop up one of the pups and carry it for a while. They tired easily since they were so small. When the sun dipped below the horizon, they made camp for the night.

It was late in the afternoon the next day as they started up the trail along the river to the Valley. The goats picked up their pace as they neared home. Soon their bleating was answered by the herd grazing in the meadow. As the group entered the Valley, they were met by Deet.

"I was beginning to worry about you. You should have been back two days ago," he said, taking the pack Yani was carrying.

"Things didn't go as I had hoped but let's get home and I can tell you all about it," she replied.

"Where did you get these two," he asked when he noticed the wolf pups. "I'm guessing that's one of the reasons you're late."

"They didn't slow us down but they are part of the story. But home first."

As they neared the village, Ami joined them. "Let me take care of the goats. You go on home. You look tired," she said. She unloaded the packs from the goats before she led them toward the pasture.

Cru gave Yani a hug and then said, "I'm going home." As he walked away the two wolf pups followed him.

"Make sure they don't go near the sheep or goats. There are new babies," Etta called after him. "We'll need to start training them right away. But not until tomorrow."

Cru waved as he trudged off toward his home.

"How did he do on the trip?" asked Deet. "I think that's the first time I've ever seen that boy walk rather than run."

"He did very well," replied Etta. "He never complained. Not even when we walked most of the night. But let's get inside and as we eat, we can tell you."

They had just gotten settled around the fire pit when Dami and Dorf called, "May we enter?"

"Of course," called Yani. "You'll probably need to hear our news too. "

Dami , Yani's younger sister, was carrying a pot of stew as she came down the steps into Yani's house. She placed it on the fire to stay warm then joined Etta on one of the sleeping benches.

"That sounds serious. Should I get the others?" asked Dorf.

"No, not yet. I would like for you to hear what I have to say then we can decide if there's concern or if I've overreacted," replied Yani. "But first we need to eat."

As soon as she and Etta had a bowl of stew, she began her story. "When we got near my old home Wolf began growling his warning growl. I sent Etta, Cru, and the goats to hide in the dunes as Wolf and I moved nearer to see what was troubling him. What I found were three men collecting flint from the beach. I don't know why the sight of them troubled me so much but I sensed there was something not right. I decided not to risk an encounter with them and moved back to where I had left Etta and Cru. We stayed hidden in the dunes all that night and most of the next day before the strange men finally left. After they were gone, we went on up the beach and as quickly as possible collected the flint I would need. We had planned to spend the night there but what we found in Birg's cave changed my mind. Cru was exploring the beach while I fixed us a warm supper. Remember we had been mainly just eating jerky as we traveled, then again as we hid. Anyway, he not only found those two wolf pups but the mother, too. She had been killed but not skinned. Why would men leave a wolf pelt? And it looked like they had killed her by hitting her over the head with a rock. It was as if they didn't have spears. There were just too many things about this that troubled me.

"Instead of spending the night, as soon as we had eaten, we packed up and started back. There was a full moon so it made walking easy. To be safe we walked in the wet sand so that the tide would cover our tracks. I knew the tide would come back in before dawn. We walked until it was clear Cru couldn't go on, then we made camp and slept. The sun had come up when we woke. As soon as we could we moved on, but we were all so tired that we stopped early the next day."

"Do you have any idea who these men were or where they came from?" asked Dorf.

"No," she replied. "I didn't think of it until we were too far to go back or I would have looked to see if they had settled in the meadow. It may have recovered enough from the fire by now that you could live there again."

"Maybe Holt and Dorf should go check it out," suggested Dami.

"That's a good idea but if I know Holt he'll want to go alone," said Dorf. Although they were brothers the men were quite different. Dorf stayed mostly in the Valley, hunting in the nearby woods. Holt was a wanderer. He ranged far and wide hunting, trapping, and fishing. In his travels he also collected seeds from the plants he came across, planting them in the Valley to discover what would make a decent food crop. He was the one who should go investigate because he could move quickly and silently through the woods.

"I'll go have a talk with him," said Dorf.

# Chapter Seven

Holt left the Valley just before dawn. He moved swiftly down the river to the shore then turned north toward Yani's beach. When the sun came up, he was well on his way up the coast. He walked steadily all day and had passed the camp by the stream shortly after the sun was at its highest. When night caught him, he was a half day from Yani's beach. He made a cold camp and rolled up in his sleeping cloak.

Before the sun was at its zenith the next day, he was nearing his destination. Instead of continuing on he turned inland into the scrub brush that had returned after the fire had destroyed the forest. Moving slowly and silently he made his way to the edge of the meadow. Using a clump of small pine trees for cover he scanned the meadow. What he found was a crude lean-to resting against the remains of one of the houses. As he watched two men emerged from the lean-to and added some wood to the fire that was smoldering there. Shortly after, one of the men sat down and picked a flint nodule from a pile by the fire.

"You're never going to make a blade," said the other man. "I still think the best thing we can do is grab that girl who lived with the Knapper. The rumor is he taught her how to make blades."

"And how are we supposed to grab her? We don't know where she is. Or even if she is still alive." the first man replied "I mean how hard can it be. If a measly girl can do it."

The second man just shook his head and went back into the lean-to while the first man continued to work on the flint. Each time he struck off a flake he would hold it up and examine it. Most he just threw into a pile off to one side but occasionally he would seem to be pleased with one and place it in a different pile. Holt watched the lean-to until the sun started to sink behind the hills in the west. He slipped back into the scrub brush and moved off. When he had gone far enough that he felt safe he stopped and made a camp for the night. Then he slept.

The next morning, he was back at the camp watching. This time he had circled around the meadow and was in the brush close to the stream. He knew the men would have to come for water some time and then he would be able to get a better look at them. The sun was high in the sky when one of them crawled out of the lean-to and stumbled to the stream. After splashing water on his face, he drank his fill then stood and stretched. As Holt predicted he stood looking out over the returning forest facing him. With a good look at his face, Holt was able to verify what he expected. The two parallel scars across his face confirmed that he was an outlaw. His village chief had banished him for some crime against the village. The scars warned other villages that he was not someone they should welcome into their village. Without the support of one's village an outlaw often did not survive. Yani's father had been banished from his village for his harsh treatment of her mother. Holt had been sent to track him and make sure he was not going to be a threat to Yani. Holt found him. It was clear he would not bother Yani. Nor would he ever harm anyone again since a bear had killed him.

Holt continued to watch for the rest of the day. As the sun set, he had managed to get a good look at all three of the men. They all bore the scars of an outlaw although one's scars were not as distinct as the other two. As the light faded Holt slipped back into the underbrush and began his journey back toward the village.

# Chapter Eight

Holt took a round-about route back to the Valley. It was late afternoon two days later when he walked out of the woods into the village. Cru spotted him as he emerged and alerted the whole village. "Holt's home! Holt's home!" the boy called as he ran to greet his friend.

"Nice greeting, Cru," said Holt with a grin for the boy. "And what if I wanted to sneak up on Lamu and surprise her?"

"Oh, no, I didn't think about that," blurted the boy as he skidded to a halt. He looked at Holt a moment then grinned back. "I know, I'll run and tell her I was only kidding. That you weren't back." Holt managed to grab him before he took off to find Lamu.

"Whoa! It's okay. I was just teasing you. But you can run and find Dorf and Sven. Tell them to come to Yani's house. I need them to hear what I found out."

Holt was sitting across the fire from Deet and Yani when Dorf and Sven entered. Lamu, Honi and Dami were not far behind. Seeing that most of the village were gathered, Holt said, "It looks like Fin, Birg and Ami are the only ones missing but we can fill them in later. I'll be brief. I spent two days watching the men Yani saw on her beach. They have built a lean-to in the meadow and it appears they're trying to teach themselves how to make blades. Or at least, one of them is. Not very successfully from what I saw. And they are indeed outlaws. I got close enough to see their scars."

The group sat quietly mulling over the news. Finally, Deet said, "Then Yani can't go alone to gather nodules anymore. There's no telling what they might do."

"I agree," said Holt, "especially when you consider what I overheard. One of them said it would be easier if they did as he suggested and kidnap Yani so she could make their blades. They figured the Knapper had taught her how."

"Then I don't think she should go there at all anymore," said Deet. "And that's that."

"Don't you think I should have a say in this?" asked Yani. "I may have other ideas. After all I'm the one who needs the flint and more importantly, I'm the one in danger."

"I don't see any other option," said Deet. "You're not going there again as long as those outlaws are there."

"No, Deet. I am going again. I'm going to go and teach them how to make blades then they'll not be a danger to me."

"You are going to do what?" roared Deet as he jumped to his feet. "I…I…I.." he sputtered.

"Oh, Deet, calm down. Sit back down and listen to me. If I go, I will take Dorf, Holt and Fin with me. And also, Wolf. They would be no match for us. I will show them how to make basic blades. I can do that in a day or two. Then we will see what happens from there."

"I still don't like it," said Deet as he slumped down on the sleeping bench.

"I don't expect you do, but I've been my own person for too long to obey any man," said Yani as she glared at Deet.

They stared at each other until finally Deet broke the stare and mumbled, "Alright you win, but I'm going too."

"No, I need you to stay here and watch over the Valley. Besides, you're too hot tempered. This is going to take a calm gentle hand," said Yani as she patted him lovingly. "I will be fine."

Yani with Wolf, Fin, Dorf, and Holt for protection left the Valley early the next day on their mission. They were traveling light, just a traveling pouch with food and water for the trip and their sleeping cloaks. As they walked swiftly along the shore, Fin joined Yani. "Are you sure this is a wise thing to do?" asked the boy. "I didn't want to say anything in front of the others. What if they decide to fight us and take you anyway?"

"I've thought of that. But in the end, they would lose. I can make good blades and I also can make blades that break and wobble and all kinds of things that they wouldn't like. But with you men and Wolf I have plenty of protection. I'll teach them enough that they can hunt and not starve. Then we'll leave. Don't worry. It'll be all right," she assured the boy.

"If you say so, but I'm going to be on my guard the whole time," Fin replied.

"That's exactly what I want you to do."

They stopped for the night just south of Yani's beach. They camped there so they would arrive at the meadow the next morning before the sun rose.

It was still dark when they made their way up the cliff, through what was left of the beech forest and into the meadow. Silently, they took up places around the lean-to and waited for the outlaws to appear. The sun was halfway to its high point when the first one stumbled out. He stood squinting into the morning light then froze. "What do you want?" he asked when he saw Yani and the armed men surrounding the camp.

"I have come to teach you to make blades," said Yani. "My friends are here to see that you do me no harm while I'm teaching you."

By then the other two had heard the voices and joined the group. "You're going to voluntarily teach us to make blades?" another of the group asked. "You know we're outlaws? No one is supposed to help us. You can see our scars."

"Yes, I know you're outlaws. But I also know you're desperate and desperate men do desperate things. If you can hunt and feed yourselves you will be less likely to do something much worse than what you were banished for. So do you want to learn or not?"

"Yes," said the one who had been trying to teach himself. "I want to learn."

"All right," said Yani, "let's get started." She dropped down by the fire and began looking through the pile of flints they had collected. The man who had indicated he wanted to learn sat down beside her. "My name is…" he started but Yani stopped hm.

"I don't want to know your name. We are not to be friends. I will call you Learner and you will call me Teacher. When you have learned what you need, we will leave and hopefully never see each other again. Is that understood?"

"Yes, Teacher," answered the Learner.

"And do either of you others want to learn, too?" asked Yani.

They just looked at her and shook their heads. "Then while I am here you will remain in your lean-to where we can keep an eye on you. Is that clear?"

They started to protest. One started to take a step toward Yani when Wolf stepped forward growling. Fin raised his spear. Holt and Dorf also stepped forward. The outlaw froze then mumbling turned and crawled into the lean-to without another word.

Turning to the Learner, Yani began her instruction. "The first thing is to select the right flint nodule. This one is not a good one. The shape is wrong and see this discoloration, that is a weak spot. Now this one," Yani said picking up a different nodule, "is a good one. This flattened area makes it easy to stabilize while you work it. Next you take your hammer stone and hit it…"

The lesson continued until the late afternoon. By then the Learner had progressed enough that Yani felt he could eventually teach himself to make usable blades. Not of a quality that he could trade them but they would be good enough to hunt with. Yani stood and stretched. "You have the basics. Now you need to practice. Either you will get better or you won't. That's up to you."

"I don't know how I can thank you, Teacher," said the Learner. "You have probably saved our lives."

"You can thank me by taking your friends and leaving my meadow. I have no problem with you coming here to collect flint from time to time but I would rather you not live here."

"I think we can do that," he replied.

"What gives you the right to tell us where we can live," yelled one of the men from the lean-to.

"And just how did you know we were here anyway?" called the other one.

Yani just smiled at them as they glared out of the lean-to at her. "How did I know you were here? The spirit of the mother you killed told me when she brought her children to me to care for. She told me that three men too helpless to even make a spear had to bludgeon her to death with a rock. And then they were too ignorant to take her pelt. They didn't apologize to her spirit for killing her and it appeared they did it out of fear rather than need. So, since you angered the animal spirit it would probably be wise not to stay here."

Wolf had moved to her side. As she finished the hackles on his neck raised and he growled softly. Yani ran her hand over Wolf's neck and he calmed.

"We will be gone in two days," said the Learner. "I think I have a blade or two that are good enough to hunt with. As soon as we have made a kill so we can have some meat we will leave. It has been a long time since we've had red meat so we're weak. Once we've regained some strength we'll move on. And thank you. I am sorry we angered the animal spirit. We were weak and afraid."

Yani nodded to the young man and then began to walk back across the meadow toward the path to the beach. The others followed keeping an eye on the outlaw camp until they had disappeared into the beech forest. Soon the new foliage that had grown up between the few trees that had survived the fire, hid them from the outlaws' view.

When they reached the beach instead of heading toward home, they turned inland into the dunes. As soon as they had rounded the top of the highest dune they dropped to the ground where they could watch the beach. They needed to know that the outlaws weren't following them. Holt settled by Yani's side and quietly whispered, "I think you have lived with Deet too long, my friend," he said with a chuckle. "That was a good story you told."

"And what is that supposed to mean? I told it just like it was. The mother wolf left her babies where we could find them. It was obvious that someone who didn't honor the animal spirit had killed her. I didn't exactly say where she had come to me, now, did I? I think it had the right effect, didn't it?"

Holt chuckled and shook his head. "I guess you're right about that."

"I feel sorry for the young man I taught. He seems like a weak young man who got caught up with the wrong crowd. I just hope they don't turn on him before he can slip away. The other two are mean and evil. They are much like my father was."

They didn't have long to wait before the three outlaws came jogging down the path from the cliff. As they watched, two of the outlaws ran to the water's edge and looked up and down the beach.

"Where could they have gone this soon?" asked one. "Surely they couldn't have gotten out of sight in the time it took for us to catch up with them?"

As they wandered the shore looking for evidence of Yani and her friends, the Learner remained at the base of the path. As Yani watched he began dragging his feet through the sand wiping out the traces of their footprints, while watching the other two. When the traces of their tracks were wiped out, he called, "Look! Is that a boat out there? See it just at the edge of the fog bank?"

"Where? I don't see anything," called one of his comrades.

"It's just there. I can just see the top of a sail. It's straight out… No, it's gone. I guess I could see it from here since I am just a little higher than you. They must have had a boat waiting to take them away. Maybe they came with the Seapeople. You noticed that the woman was the only one who talked."

The other two walked back and forth for a while grumbling then the three turned and walked back up the path. As they reached the edge of the beech forest, the Learner turned back and waved before following his companions into the trees.

Yani and the men waited until they were sure the outlaws had gone then they started their journey back home. At first, they jogged near the edge of the water where the tide would erase their footprints. When they had gone far enough that it was safe, they moved a little higher up the beach and slowed their pace. They continued down the beach until the sky had turned dark and the moon rose over the sea. Finally, they felt it was safe to stop and rest.

# Chapter Nine

The light was fading when Yani, Holt, Dorf and Fin neared the river trail. As they approached a figure arose from the rock that marked the beginning of the trail. Seeing her Yani hurried forward to the welcome embrace of the girl.

"At last, you're back," said Etta. "We have all been so worried. I was about to talk Deet into coming with me to go see if you needed to be rescued."

"As you can see, we're fine. With such a bodyguard as I took with me, the outlaws didn't stand a chance. But we're tired. Let's get to the Village and we can tell you all the story," replied Yani.

As they entered the Village word passed quickly that Yani was safely back. By the time they had reached Yani's house most of the adults in the Village had already gathered. Seeing the crowd, Yani said, "Let's go to the big firepit and talk there. Birg, can you get a fire going there, please."

Birg nodded and hurried ahead to light the fire that was always kept in readiness for such gatherings. The others followed and soon they were all settled around the blazing fire. Before Yani started with her tale, Lamu and Honi ladled out bowls of stew to the travelers.

Once Yani had finished eating she started telling the others what had happened. "The outlaws were still there. We spent the night on the beach and were able to sneak up to the meadow and be in place when they woke up. As I suspected at least one of them wanted to learn and I taught him. The other two were worthless. The funny part was ..."

When Yani had finished her tale and had answered all their questions, the group separated and went to their homes.

As spring turned to summer Etta continued to work on her herb garden. She had found horehound, yarrow, tansy, and calamine in the woods and replanted them into her prepared ground. Each time she collected plants to dry she brought back a few starts to plant. It was slow business but eventually she would have most of the common plants that Yani needed for her medicines.

One day Ami, Birg's mate, noticed Etta standing by the goat pen watching the new kids that had been born earlier that spring. Joining her, Ami said, " They are so cute when they're this age. I never get tired of watching them frisk about."

"Yes, they are very cute but I am more interested in how strong they are," replied Etta. "Which of them do you think would make the best pack animals?"

"Are you planning on becoming a trader?" asked Ami with a chuckle. "Don't we have enough traders in this Valley with Deet and Birg wandering around most of the winter?"

"Well, I didn't have trading in mind, but I was thinking of making a trek."

"So, you're going to try to talk Deet into taking you with him this year?" asked Ami.

"This is my twelfth summer and he did promise to take me with him when I was old enough. Besides, I know Yani wants to see the Mountains That Are Always White one more time. Between you and me I'm not sure she'll be able to make the trek if we wait much longer."

The two watched the goats in silence for a while then Ami said, "I have seen that Yani is aging. How was she when you went with her to get the flint last spring?"

"Oh, she did fine then but that was a short trip in pleasant weather. I'm not sure how she would hold up on a long winter trip. From what Deet tells me it's a long hard walk," replied Etta. "And have you watched Wolf? He's aging too. I'm not sure he could make the trek and pull his traveling pack."

"So, you're thinking of training a goat to carry some of the weight?" said Ami.

"Actually, two goats. We need to keep Yani's pack as light as possible and it wouldn't hurt to lighten Deet's load, too."

"All right then let's look at these kids. You'll have your work cut out for you, you know. Maybe you can get Cru to help with the training. He's really good with the goats."

Ami and Etta finally settled on a set of twin nannies. They were sturdy black and white spotted girls. "I think you should focus on one of them at a time. As you work with one the other will follow along. I've noticed they like to be together. The first thing you need to do is get the harnesses made. Fin can help you there. He is good with working leather. Come to the house with me. I have an old deer hide sleeping cloak you can use."

As soon as Etta left Ami's house with the deer hide, she went in search of Fin. She soon found him by the river cutting willow wands to weave into fish weirs. Etta watched for a few minutes before calling out to him.

"Fin, can I talk to you for a few minutes," she said.

"Seems to me that's what you are doing," he replied with a grin. He cut a couple more wands before he stopped and joined Etta on the riverbank. "So, what's on your mind? From the look on your face I have a feeling it is going to be work for me."

"You're right. It is work. I have a favor to ask," said Etta. "Do you think you can make this into two goat harnesses like the one Birg uses with his pack goat?"

"No doubt I could but the question is why? Are you thinking of becoming a trader?"

"Of course not," said Etta. "But I want to train a couple of the new kids to be pack animals."

Fin didn't answer for a few moments. He looked Etta in the eye then finally he shook his head. "I see, you're going to try to get Deet to take you with him and you think two well trained pack goats will convince him to let you tag along when he leaves this winter. That's it isn't it?"

"Yes, I want to go with him but that is not exactly how I would have put it," said Etta indignantly. "You always see things from the worst angle possible."

"No, I see things from the most realistic angle possible."

"I want the pack goats so Yani won't have to carry a heavy pack. She wants to go to her mother's home once more while she still can."

"And you know this how?" asked Fin.

"I know this because when I first started nagging Deet she told me. And I'm afraid this winter may be her last chance. I figured if I made it as easy as possible for her, she could make it. Wolf's too old to carry much of a load so the next option would be goats. Ami and I picked out a set of twins I plan to train this summer so they will be ready to go when the time comes."

Fin stood and looked out over the river for a while. Etta knew to hold her peace while he thought it over. They had been like brother and sister since the big fire had left them orphans. She sat and watched the water drift by as Fin considered. Finally, he said, "All right, I'll make you the harnesses. I think you are wasting your time but it might work. Give me the deer hide and show me which of the kids you want to train."

"Thank you, Fin," Etta cried hugging the boy.

"Enough!" Fin mumbled as he pushed Etta way. "Come on I need to get busy on these harnesses if you're going to get them trained by summer's end." Turning away he walked off toward the goat pen with Etta in tow.

A few days later Fin found Etta planting more starts in her herb garden. "I got your harnesses done. You want to see if we can get those critters to let us put them on?" he asked her.

"Let me finish these last two plants. It'll only take a minute and I don't want them to die." Etta quickly dug two small holes and after adding a little water she set the bee balm starts in the holes and gently packed the soil around them. "Okay, let's go."

They walked down toward the goat pen in silence. When they neared the pen, Fin asked, "Are you sure you want to talk Yani into going on this trek. It might kill her, you know?"

"I'm not going to talk her into anything. I'm just going to be ready in case she wants to go. And of course, I'm going to try to talk Deet into taking me. I've wanted to go with him since I was a little girl. And he promised me that when I was twelve summers he would," replied Etta.

"If you say so," said Fin. "I still think you're crazy. I don't understand why you would want to walk all that way when we have everything we need right here."

"But think of all that you would see on the way. And can you imagine mountains that high? So high the snow never melts from them. And all the interesting people and villages you would get to know."

Fin stopped and looked down at Etta. "No, I don't want to think of them. I want to stay right here where I belong and I think you should too. But you have always been a strange one."

They walked in silence until they reached the goat pen. "There's the two I mean," said Etta pointing to the twins. She climbed over the fence into the pen. As soon as they noticed her the two kids came running. She knelt down to nuzzle them both as Fin caught up with her.

Fin soon had the harnesses fitted on the kids. He made a few adjustments so they fit snuggly and didn't rub. "See how I made these loops here," he said pointing out where he had slipped the straps through a double loop of leather. "As they grow you can move the loops forward making it a little bigger so it will always fit. Just be sure to tighten it like this."

"That's very clever. I was wondering what I would do if they outgrew their harnesses. And the baskets will hang here on these straps down their side, right?" said Etta.

"You know that. You've seen Stinker's harness often enough," grumbled Fin

"Don't be cross, Fin. You know how long I've wanted this," said Etta quietly.

"It's just that we've lost all the rest of our family. I don't want to lose you."

"What do you mean? We have a whole village of family. They all love us like their own," said Etta.

"You know what I mean," pleaded Fin.

"No, I don't know what you mean. When the fire killed our parents Yani, Lamu and Loki became mothers to us. And Deet, Birg and Han were just like fathers. We never wanted for a home. And why would you think that you would lose me. I'm coming back at the end of the trek just like Deet does. You're not going to lose me," insisted Etta.

"But what if something happens to you. Or if something happens to Deet and you can't find your way back?" asked Fin.

"What if you fall in the river and drown? What if you run into a bear and it kills you? Something could happen any place. Yes, I could get killed but I don't plan on it. I plan on coming back here and telling you of all kinds of wonderful things I have seen along the way. But now let's get busy with these kids and start training them," Etta said as she hugged Fin.

# Chapter Ten

As the leaves began to turn the dull dark green that told her summer was ending, Etta started preparing for the trek. It had been a summer's long battle trying to convince Deet that he should take Yani and her with him on his winter journey. She smiled as she recalled the ongoing battle.

"Etta, for the last time I am not going to take Yani on this fool's errand. And what makes you think she even wants to go?" stormed Deet when Etta had brought it up as they were carrying the dried fish back from the beach. Deet had been preparing for his trading journey all summer and now it was time to start packing.

"Come on, Deet, you know she wants to see her mother's village again. And she was just reminiscing about Gyla as we gathered witch hazel twigs a couple of days ago. I know she can make the trip. Especially if she doesn't have to carry a load," coaxed Etta.

"I should have known you were up to something when I saw you harnessing up those two kids. But I never thought this was what you had planned."

"Please, Deet, you did promise you would take me with you when I was twelve summers. Don't you remember?" pleaded Etta.

"And that was one of the dumbest things I have ever done in my long stupid life. For the last time, NO," shouted Deet as he walked on ahead.

Later that evening as they were sitting down to a bowl of rabbit stew, Etta casually said, "I wonder if your uncle is still alive. The one who was so nice to you when you and the Knapper visited on his last trading journey."

Etta kept her eyes on her stew but could feel Deet's glare across the fire. "I would imagine he has already passed over to the Otherside by now. He was older than I was," said Deet.

"Oh, I am fairly sure he would still be alive. He's not that much older than we are. And yes, Etta, it would be nice to go see him. As a matter of fact, I was just thinking about that the other day. I think this winter may be the right time for that trip you promised us so long ago. When do you plan to leave, Deet? I have things I need to put in order before we start out."

Etta chuckled to herself as she remembered Deet's reaction when Yani said she wanted to make the trip. But he gave in as he always did when Yani wanted something. Now she was nearly finished with the preparation for the long trip. They would spend the coming winter moving south, stopping at villages and trading along the way. By spring they would be crossing the Steppes, a wide sea of grass that divided the northern forests from the Mountains That Are Always White. They would spend the next summer resting and preparing for a long winter's walk back to the Valley. Etta had always wanted to go with Deet, but now that it was a reality, the thought of being away from Fin, Cru, and the rest of the people she loved for so long was a bit frightening.

Etta had an assortment of herbs laid out on an old deer hide in the sun. Before she packed them in the small hide bags she had made, she wanted to make sure they were thoroughly dried. Once she had them dried to her satisfaction, she would bag them and put them in a larger pouch before stowing them in one of the baskets the goats would carry. The goats had been easier to train than she had expected. Before the summer was half over, she had them both carrying a light load as she gathered plants in the forests. Whenever she went to the beach to look for mussels and crabs, or clams that she just recently discovered were good to eat, she took one of the goats to carry her find back. Now that the summer was ending, she followed Birg's advice and was also putting rocks in the bottom of the basket to add weight. They needed to toughen up in order to carry the heavy load they would need to carry on the trek south.

She mused over all that needed to be done as she sorted her herbs. Soon she became aware she was being watched. Without stopping her work, she said, "Cru, I know you're there so you might as well come over here and help me."

"How do you always know when I'm sneaking up on you?" the boy said, "I try to be real quiet."

"You may try but you don't succeed," laughed Etta. "Come here and sit by me while I bag up these herbs."

"I wish you would take me, too," he said as he joined her. "I'm strong enough to make the trip. I know I could do it!"

"Do you remember how far it was to go to Yani's beach last spring? And how tired you got before we got back home?" asked Etta.

Cru nodded and started to object, "Yes, but I…"

"No 'yes buts.' This trip is going to be like that everyday all winter. We may stop from time to time to trade in a village but for the most part we will be walking and walking. We will get cold and tired and probably also hungry. And once we get started there is no going back. Do you understand?"

"I know it will be a long trip and it will be hard but I still want to go. I want to see all the things that you see," said Cru.

"What will Dan and your mother do without you? And how will Ami manage to take care of all the goats. She says you are her best helper," said Etta.

"Please, Etta," begged the boy, "Ask Deet to take me, too."

"No Cru, I won't do that. And besides, I know already what he will say. A big fat NO. Now if you're not going to help me, go someplace else and stop pestering me.."

With one more pleading look, Cru began helping put the herbs in the bags. By the time they were done his usual cheerful nature had returned and he was chattering away as they carried the pouch of herbs to Yani's house.

The summer had ended and the traders were beginning to load up for their trading journeys. Birg had already left on the first of his short circuits. Since he and Ami had become Life Mates, he went on several short loops to the villages where he traded. In between he would spend some time at home in the Valley.

Deet was still a trader who spent the winter traveling and only returning to the Valley in the summer. Etta noticed though that the past few seasons he had been leaving later in the fall and returning earlier in the spring. She wasn't sure if it was because he tired more easily now or that he missed Yani and the comforts of home. She realized this was going to be a hard trek for Deet too. She wished she could have talked Fin into coming along. It would be nice to have a strong young man in case there was a problem. But then she thought if Yani, when she was eleven summers, and the old Knapper could make the trip then surely they would do fine.

The morning before they were due to leave, she checked the supplies in the baskets one last time. They had a good supply of salt that she had helped Birg make. It was in small bags that were the right size for trading. She had put a few of them in each of the four baskets that would go on the goats as well as in the packs each of them would carry. It made sense to do this so if they got caught in a bad storm the odds were against losing all the salt. Also, it would even up the loads. She did however make sure that she had only put a few in Yani's pack as the salt was the heaviest thing they were taking with them. In the pack she would be carrying she had put the small bag holding the pieces of amber she had found on the shore. That was the most precious item they had to trade. Among the other trade goods were the dried fish from the sea which had a salty taste and were oilier than the fish from the lakes and rivers inland. They had the dried herbs, some dried vegetables, the flint blades Yani made and some of the whale fat they traded with the Seapeople for. This last, they would save to use in an emergency. If they got caught in a snowstorm it could provide energy that would help ward off the cold. Most of the food items they would eat along the way, but some they would also trade for what they needed as they traveled. Satisfied that all was in readiness, she started her round of the village to say her goodbyes.

# Part 2

# The Journey South

# Chapter One

The sun had yet to peek above the horizon as the travelers began their journey. They had said their goodbyes the night before so they could slip away quietly. It had only taken a few minutes to harness and load up the goats. Their packs were loaded and waiting by the door. After a breakfast of the left-over porridge from the night before they were on their way.

"I'm glad Lamu offered to wash up from our breakfast," said Etta as they left the Valley and entered the forest. "I know it would have only taken a few minutes for me to do it before we left but still it's nice to just eat and be on our way."

"It'll be an exhausting day so the early start will help," answered Yani. "This will allow us to rest more often today. After a few days on the trail, we'll toughen up. By then we should be able to walk all day with only a stop to eat."

"I'm not in a hurry so we can rest when you like. Neither of us are as young as we used to be. I just hope we don't regret this," added Deet.

"I'm sure I can make it all the way but I'm not sure of my friend here," said Yani as she lovingly laid her hand on Wolf's head. As usual he was walking close by her side.

"We are both a couple of old men, aren't we, Wolf," chuckled Deet. "But I think we can make one more journey south."

Midmorning they stopped for a rest by a spring that bubbled out of the cliff at the edge of the path they had been following. They drank their fill from the cool clear water. Yani passed small pieces of jerked elk to each of them, including Wolf. As they rested, Wolf kept looking back down the trail the way they had just come.

"Are you regretting coming with us already, Wolf?" asked Etta. "I noticed he's been looking back a lot. Almost as if we were being followed."

"If someone were following us, he would be more protective. I think he is just hoping we'll turn back so he can lay in the sun and sleep. You've gotten lazy in your old age, haven't you," said Deet. "Still, I'm going to keep an eye out behind us just in case. I'm still uncomfortable knowing those outcasts could still be in the area."

For most of the day they followed a narrow trail between the cliff and the river. The further from the Valley they traveled the steeper the cliff became until it towered over them. The river had changed from the gentle slow-moving stream that crossed their valley to roaring rapids. It was so loud that they had to yell to be heard. Toward evening the path began to climb, switch backing up the cliff until it reached an oak covered plateau. Here the trail left the river and turned southwest. The trail widened here making the going easier. They stopped for a short rest now that they were away from the roar of the water. There had been no good stopping places along the river path so as they rested Etta handed out jerky and dried blackberries for a late lunch.

"Wolf, come here," said Deet. "We're not going back to the river. If you're thirsty you're just going to have to wait until we get to the camp site tonight. It's not very far. We should be there before dark." Wolf looked at Deet and whined. "What is your problem, old boy?"

"He is acting strangely. But not like he would act if there was danger," said Yani.

"Maybe he'll settle down once we get a little further from home," suggested Etta.

It was twilight when they reached the campsite. It was obvious it was a popular place to camp as there was a well-built firepit and someone had even left a small pile of dead wood to get a fire going. While Deet started a fire, Etta fetched water from the babbling brook that ran at the edge of the campsite. When she got back Yani had unharnessed the goats and they were grazing on the tuffs of grass here and there around the camp. They soon had a pot of acorn meal porridge bubbling on the fire. Yani added a few bits of dried fish to add some flavor. As soon as they had eaten, Etta took the pot to the brook and washed it. As she was returning to the camp, she heard a twig snap back along the trail they had just traveled. Wolf looked up at her as if to say see I told you so. She looked into the fading light but could see nothing. After waiting a bit to see if she would hear any other movement, she decided it had just been some forest animal.

Soon the tired travelers were fast asleep rolled in their sleeping cloaks.

As the sun broke through the canopy of oak leaves the travelers woke and prepared for the day. Etta stirred up the fire to cook their breakfast porridge. Deet and Yani harnessed the goats and got their packs on. As soon as they had eaten, they were on their way.

The sun was high in the sky when Deet moved up beside Etta on the trail. In a quiet voice, he said, "I don't want to alarm you but Wolf is right. We are being followed. In a little while the trail will take a sharp turn to the left and pass through some big rocks. When it does anyone following will not be able to see us on the trail up ahead. As soon as we are out of sight, I am going to duck behind the rocks and wait. I don't want whoever it is sneaking up on us during the night. I don't think there is a threat or Wolf would be warning us. But just in case."

"All right. I'll let Yani know what is happening and we'll keep Wolf with us," said Etta. "Just be careful."

"I will," replied Deet.

Just as Deet said, the trail took a sharp turn not long after. Yani and Etta with the animals kept walking as Deet slipped off the trail behind the rocks. They had only gone a short distance down the trail when they heard Deet's yell followed by a scream. Yani looked at Etta and said, "Should we go back?"

"I don't think that will be necessary. I recognized that scream," replied Etta with a big grin. "Deet should be here in a moment with our stalker."

Sure enough, it was only a few minutes later that Deet came walking down the trail with a grip on the arm of his catch. When Yani saw who it was she just shook her head. "What on earth are you doing here, Cru? You can't be thinking that we would take you with us now, were you?"

"Please! I want to go, too. I know I can make the trip and I would be a big help. I can gather grass for the goats. I can trap rabbits. I can carry part of your load. And besides its too far to go back now," pleaded Cru.

"I have a mind to turn you around and make you go back on your own but I suspect you would just keep on following us. I don't know what to do with you. What will your parents think when they find you missing?" said Deet.

# Chapter Two

The day before the traders were set to leave, Cru had taken Dan aside. "I have a secret I need to tell you but you have to promise not to tell anybody, at least not right away. Do you promise?" asked Cru.

"That depends. Is this something that will get me in trouble like you usually do? Because if so, no, I won't keep your secret," answered his friend.

"No, you won't get in trouble. But if you tell too soon I sure will. So do you promise?" asked Cru.

"I guess. But I don't like it."

"Okay. Here's my plan. I sneaked a pack with what I would need and have it hidden in the woods by the trail. Tomorrow when Yani, Deet and Etta leave I'm going to follow them," started Cru.

"You are going to do what? Are you crazy? Don't answer. Of course, you're crazy," yelled Dan.

"Sssh! Not so loud. It's not crazy. All I have to do is follow them along the path. If I can get a day or two along it will be too late for them to bring me back. And I really don't think they would send be back on my own. All I need you to do is to wait until they miss me and then tell Mother and Father. It will be dark before anyone thinks to look for me since I am a wanderer anyway. I think it'll work."

"And what are you going to do about Black. You have him almost trained. You can't go off and leave him but he would give you away if you took him,"

"Yeah, well, that's the other thing. Would you keep him? I really hate to leave him but I want to go on this trip more. Before I go, I'll tie him in the cave that the sheep stay in during the winter. I'll leave him some food so he will be okay until you get up and untie him. I should be long gone by then."

"I guess. But I still think you're crazy," mumbled Dan.

"Thank you. You are my best friend," said Cru, giving Dan a hug.

"I'm your only friend, you dope," replied Dan with a grin.

The following morning as Yani, Deet and Etta started down the trail another traveler slipped from the village, too. He had already tied his wolf pup in the cave and was in the woods waiting as the traders walked by. He waited long enough to give them a head start before following them down the trail.

Dami had the morning porridge ready when she realized Cru was not there. "Where is Cru," she asked Dorf.

He looked up from the blade he was attaching to a spear shaft and said, "I'm guessing he woke up hungry and made the rounds of the neighbors until he found someone who he could con into feeding him. He'll be alright. He is smart enough not to leave the Valley. He'll turn up sometime today. That smells good."

But he didn't turn up.

Dan went to the cave and released Black as soon as he could slip away. He had his wolf pup, Gray, with him so Black was content to play with his brother. Dan hoped that he would continue to be content and not wander off looking for Cru. It was going to be a long, difficult day for Dan.

Near midday Dan wandered down to the river where Fin was setting fish weirs. He stood on the bank watching for a while then asked, "Fin, if you promise someone something is it ever okay to break that promise?"

Without looking up, Fin said, "No, if you make a promise then you have to keep it. What kind of friend would you be it you didn't? I mean, could your friend ever trust you again."

"That's what I was afraid of," said Dan.

Fin continued tying off his weir then said, "Of course, if that promise..." He looked up to find Dan halfway across the meadow. "I guess the answer satisfied him," muttered Fin before turning to the next weir.

It was nearly dark when Cru's absence was finally noticed. Dorf had made the rounds of all the neighbors. Soon it dawned on him that no one had seen Cru at all that day. He saw Dan sitting alone down by the goat pen and decided if anyone knew where his son was it would be Dan. He had almost reached the goat pen when Dan saw him coming. Dorf was surprised when Dan jumped up and headed for the woods. Dorf took off running after him and grabbed him just as he was ready to duck into a thicket.

"Where do you think you are going, Dan?" asked Dorf "I need to talk to you."

"He made me do it," cried Dan. "He made me promise not to tell."

"Not to tell what?" asked Dorf.

"He followed Yani, Deet and Etta. He wanted to go with them."

"Are you saying my son is all alone following behind the traders? When did he leave?"

"He had a pack in the woods and as soon as they left, he followed. I told him he was crazy. But he made me promise not to tell until you started looking for him. I wanted to tell sooner but I promised."

"And you thought that was all right. To let him wander off alone into the woods and not tell his parents. What were you thinking?" yelled Dorf.

"Is there a problem?" asked Sven as he came to see why Dorf was so angry with his son. "Has Dan done something wrong?"

"No, something foolish but probably what I would have done at his age. It's my son who has done something wrong. That darn fool kid has followed Yani, Deet and Etta," explained Dorf.

"Oh, dear, when did he leave?" asked Sven.

"As near as I can tell before dawn. He had a pack hidden in the woods," said Dorf. Looking at the setting sun, he continued, "It's too late to go after him tonight but first light I am off to get him. When I get my hands on that boy…" said Dorf.

"I'll go with you," said Sven. "They can't have gotten far. And who knows we may meet up with Deet bringing him back before midmorning."

"I'll welcome your company. And I may need you with me to keep me from skinning him alive when I catch him," said Dorf.

"I'm sorry," said Dan. "I guess I should have told."

""It's not your fault. He should never have made you promise," said Dorf.

"But if he hadn't told me, you wouldn't have known where he went," said Dan.

"That's true," replied Dorf. "Let me go tell his mother. She is going to be frantic until we can catch that imp."

# Chapter Three

"Cru, what on earth were you thinking?" asked Deet for the hundredth time. "Did you think we would just let you join us and not send you back?"

"Yes," mumbled the boy. "I figured if I got this far you would let me come."

"What are we going to do with him, Yani?" asked Deet. "I guess I could leave you here with Etta and take him back. I think I could get him back to the Valley and back to you in a day and a half."

"Let's think about it," said Yani.

"What's to think about? He can't come with us. He would never make it!" shouted Deet.

"Now calm down. I'm not saying we should take him. I'm just saying we should calm down and think it through. For starters I think we should have something to eat. Have you had anything to eat since you left the Valley yesterday, Cru?"

"A little jerky but some porridge would be really nice," said Cru hopefully.

"Then I think we should make some porridge and think," replied Yani.

They had stopped in a clearing near a stream when Deet caught back up to them. As Etta went for water, Yani gathered some rocks to make a temporary fire pit. As soon as Etta came back with some water, she helped Cru gather some wood for the fire.

"I can't believe you. We have a runaway here on our hands and you're calmly making porridge. Is everyone crazy!" yelled Deet.

"Well, Dan says I am and he is probably right," said Cru.

"Oh, Deet, sit down. As soon as we have fed this child you can take him back. If Etta and I are going to camp here and wait for you we will need a fire pit. So just calm down," said Yani. Then turning to Cru, she continued, "And yes you are going to go back.

And I agree with Dan you are crazy. You are going back not because I think you couldn't make the trip. I did it when I was only a couple summers older than you but because your parents must be frantic."

"But Dan will have told them by now. I think they will want me to go with you," said Cru, hopefully.

The other three just looked at him. Shaking her head Yani handed him a bowl of porridge.

It was late in the afternoon when they had finished eating. Etta took the bowls to the brook to wash them. The other three sat in silence by the fire.

"Deet, it is nearly dark so I think it best for you to wait until morning to start back with Cru. If you leave now, you will be getting to the narrow part of the trail along the cliff after you have lost the light. I know you are both surefooted as goats but in the dark it would be easy to trip. I'd hate for either of you to fall in the river," said Yani.

"I think…" started Cru.

"No, Cru, you don't think. Or we wouldn't be in this predicament," said Deet, glaring at the boy.

"Maybe I should go help Etta," said Cru.

As he walked off toward the stream, Yani said, "You can stop scolding him now Deet, I think he has gotten the message. I can just imagine you doing something like this when you were his age. I seem to remember some tales the Knapper told of just such pranks."

"I never did anything this stupid," mumbled Deet. "But you are right. I think I've given him a hard time long enough. I just hate to think of the time we'll have lost by taking him back."

"We have nothing but time now Deet. It won't matter in the long run."

Etta and Cru gathered firewood to last them the night before the light had faded. They ate a cold supper of jerky since they had eaten the porridge so late in the afternoon. They were sitting around the fire listening to the sounds of the coming night when Wolf got to his feet and started to whine.

"Now what is it, Wolf?" asked Yani. "Please don't tell me that Dan has decided to follow us, too."

Wolf walked a few steps back down the trail. He stopped and looked back toward Yani wagging his tail. She had just stood up when a bundle of black fur barreled into the clearing.

"Black," cried Cru. "I told Dan to keep you tied up until I was long gone."

"And he did just that," said Dorf as he and Sven walked into the clearing. "I should skin you alive for this crazy stunt."

"But I really, really want to go with them," said Cru. "I knew if I asked, you'd say no but if I was already gone it would be too late to stop me."

"Well, it turns out I'm not too late to stop you," replied Dorf.

"Join us," said Yani. "If you are hungry, I'll be happy to make you something to eat."

"I'm fine," answered Dorf. "We have been eating jerky as we traveled. How about you, Sven?"

"I'm fine too."

The two men squatted by the fire warming their hands. "Since it is so late, we may as well spend the night with you and start back in the morning," said Dorf. "Do I have to tie you to a tree to keep you from running off again or can I trust you to stay put?"

"I won't run off," said Cru.

"If you do you will be in more trouble than you can even imagine," replied his father.

As the fire died down the group settled in for the night. As soon as Cru was sound asleep curled up with Black, Yani whispered to Dorf, "What would you think if I asked to take Cru with us?"

"I never thought you were crazy, Yani. He would be nothing but trouble. I'm not even sure he could walk that far."

"Oh, he could make the walk, I have no doubt of that. You see, I understand how he feels. I remember how much I wanted to travel when I was his age. I didn't think it would ever be possible since I was a girl but then the Knapper took me with him. Just think about it. He planned his escape so well. He had a pack which had almost everything he will need. He's only missing a few things like enough food for the trip. He brought some but he will need more. He made sure that someone would let you know where he had gone. He even made plans for Black to be cared for. I'd say for a boy of his summers he had managed this fairly well."

"He did at that. It's just surprising that Dan didn't tell on him sooner," said Dorf. "So, Yani, are you saying you would be willing to take him with you?"

"Yes, Dorf, that's what I am saying. I didn't want to talk to you in front of the boy, but if you are agreeable, I think we should give in to him."

"Let me sleep on it," replied Dorf.

"You do that. Now I have to convince Deet. He may not be so easy to persuade. But that can wait until morning when he's in a better mood." And with that Yani rolled up in her sleeping cloak and was soon sleeping soundly.

The next morning as the traders were getting the goats packed, Dorf pulled Yani aside. "Are you still of the same mind you were last night?"

"Yes, if you're willing," said Yani.

"Then he can go. His mother is going to kill me but I think you are right. If he can plan it out as well as he did then he may be ready for such a journey. Do you want to tell him or should I?"

"Maybe I should tell Deet first. I never got around to that last night. Then you can tell him."

Yani took Deet's hand and led him out of earshot of the group. Etta watched this exchange wondering what was going on. Yani whispered to Deet for a few moments then Deet exploded.

"You want to what! Are you totally crazy? Yani I can't believe this."

Moving closer so she could hear Yani, Etta realized Yani was telling him she planned to take Cru with them. "Yani, that's a great idea. Please Deet, I'll make sure he stays out of trouble. I know he can make the trip. He's a really good walker," cried Etta.

Looking over at Dorf, Deet asked, "And you are okay with this?"

Dorf looked over at his son who was watching the exchange with interest, "Yes, Deet, I agree with Yani. The gods know how I'm going to survive the wrath of his mother when I tell her but, yes, he can go."

When it dawned on Cru that his father had just given him permission to go with them, he ran over and hugged him. "I can go! You mean it?" cried the boy.

"Look at me, Cru. You know it will be two winters before we see each other again. You will have to do as Deet and Yani say as if they are your parents."

"Yes, I will do as they say. I promise," replied the boy.

"One other thing," said Dorf.

"Anything," promised Cru.

"Don't you think you should hear it before you promise?" asked his father with a grin.

"No, I'll promise anything if I can just go," replied the boy.

"It's not such a bad 'thing'. I want you to take Black with you and finish training him. Is that agreeable."

"Yes, that's perfect," said Cru giving his father another hug.

# Chapter Four

After three days on the trail, Yani's group arrived at the first village. As it happens it was Yani's old home, the Village with the Well. It had been many summers since she had last visited here. After Dami and Kali had left the village to join their lifemate, she had come twice to see her mother. But when her mother passed to the Otherside there was no longer any reason for her to make the difficult journey. Before they entered the village, they stopped to make sure Cru had Black well under control.

"I know you hate to tie him but the wealth of this village is their sheep. We can't have Black attacking them," explained Yani.

"But he never bothers our sheep or goats anymore. I taught him that first thing," protested Cru.

"Yes," said Yani, "and he now thinks of them as his pack. These are strangers so he may think of them as game. Just for the time we are here, you'll need to keep him on a lead. If each time we're in a village with livestock you do, this he will soon learn that they are not to eat."

"Okay, but I wish I didn't have to," replied Cru.

"I know but that is how I had to train Wolf," replied Yani.

Wolf gave a quiet bark as if to agree with her.

As they crossed the common area in the center of the village, she was pleased to see the well was still in good shape. She wasn't sure who the head man was now since Teek would be much too old to lead, if he were even still alive. The fact that the well had been cared for showed the headman was a good one.

As they neared the headman's house, Yani asked, "Deet, do you know who the head man is here now?"

"I thought I had told you," replied Deet. "Teek's son took his father's place several summers ago. It turns out that Mat's as good as his father was. You may not remember him since he was born after you left."

When they reached the large house that served as the village meeting place as well as the home of the headman, Deet called out, "Hello the house. May we enter?"

"Come," called a voice from within. Yani felt like she had been transported back in time when she entered. She had so many memories of being in this house. Not all of them were pleasant. As soon as her eyes adjusted to the lack of light, she was surprised to see Teek sitting on the back sleeping bench. When he saw Yani he rose and came to embrace her. "Yani, it has been such a long time. Welcome to my son's house," said Teek as he gave her a big hug.

"Now, Father, we have had this conversation before. It's still your house. I just happen to have taken over as headman. But you still are head of the house," scolded Mat. Then turning to the visitors, he said, "Welcome Deet. Since Father only has a welcome for Yani it seems. And who are these other two travelers?"

"This is Etta. She has been pestering me to take her on a trading trip since she was small. And this imp is Cru. We'll tell the story of how he happens to be with us around the fire tonight."

"Sit. Rest. Ana has a good stew on the fire. Once you have eaten, we will welcome hearing the news," said Mat.

During the evening others from the village dropped by to hear the news. Several of the villagers remembered Yani so they wanted to bid her welcome. Finally, when it was late and the stream of visitors had stopped, Mat said, "It's late. I'm sure you're tired. Yani, your old home is empty at the moment and we have been using it for guests. I think you will find everything you need there." And taking a burning brand from the fire he handed it to Deet. "I am sure Yani knows the way."

Bidding them goodnight, Yani led the way across the common to the house she had lived in until the day the Knapper had traded a handful of blades to her father for her. When she entered the house, it felt strange to be here. There was a fire laid in the firepit so she just had to touch the brand to it to light it.

"So how does it feel to be here," asked Deet as they settled on the sleeping benches for the night.

"I'm not sure. I have warm feelings for my mother but also very cold feelings for my father. It's very strange to be here in my old house," she replied.

"It has been a long day. Rest peacefully," he said. He kissed her lightly on the cheek then curled around her and was soon asleep.

Yani didn't find sleep as quickly as her traveling companions did. She lay awake reliving memories of her life here. It was nearing morning when she jerked awake with a cry. Sitting up she looked confused as to where she was.

"Are you alright?" whispered Etta from across the fire. "I heard you cry out."

"I'm fine," she replied, "it was just a nightmare."

"Do you want to talk about it?" asked Etta as she moved to Yani's side.

Wrapping her sleeping cloak around herself, Yani whispered, "Let's go outside. I don't want to wake the others."

They slipped out the door and settled on the bench just outside. The sky was beginning to lighten in the east. Once they were settled Yani told Etta about her dream. "I was a little girl again. I had taken some clover I had picked to the sheep and somehow had left the gate open. They had wondered off and Father found Wolf eating them. He had his spear poised to kill Wolf when I came upon them. I grabbed his spear to stop him and he turn around to attack me. He was jabbing the spear toward me when I screamed and woke up."

"I can see why you screamed. But it's all right now. He's gone and can't hurt you ever again," said Etta as she wrapped her arms around Yani. "You're trembling. That must have been a terrible dream. I don't think I have ever seen you this frightened."

"It was so real," replied Yani. "He was such a mean man. He came very close to killing my mother. It may be evil but I'm glad he's gone."

They sat in silence and watched the dawn break When the village started to wake up, they went back into the house to prepare for the day of trading.

# Chapter Five

Etta sat in the sun on the bench where she and Yani had watched the sunrise after Yani's nightmare. Yani had left the house early and Etta guessed she had gone to visit with Teek and his family. Deet was trading and visiting with his friends here in the village. Cru was playing with Black by the well. It was nice to just sit thought Etta. As she watched Cru playing, she couldn't help but wonder if they had made a mistake bringing the boy. So far, he had kept up with them and never complained even when he had to be tired. Watching him she suddenly realized he was wearing light weight summer moccasins. They would never do when the snows came. And he needed a warm parka or at least a vest. Rising she went in search of Deet.

Yani and Wolf were also enjoying the sunshine. They were visiting all the places that held fond memories for Yani. They had walked out to the sheep fold and watched them for a while. The flock had increased enough that besides providing wool for clothing they could harvest the young rams to provide a steady source of meat. The hunger she often knew as a child would not haunt the children of the village now.

When Etta found Deet she waited patiently until he had finished with the trade he was working on. When he had sealed his bargain, she motioned for him to come with her away from the crowd waiting to trade. When they had moved out of earshot she began. "Deet, I think we have a problem with Cru."

"Now, you decide that. I have said that all along. Although he has done a good job of keeping up," he replied. Looking over to where the boy and wolf pup were playing, he continued, "And I have to say he doesn't complain even when the going gets rough. So, what is the problem?"

"Look at what he is wearing. He will get frostbitten feet with those light summer moccasins. And he has no vest or parka," said Etta.

"You're right. How could Yani and I have missed that. I guess we are both getting old and forgetful," replied Deet.

"I am wondering if I could take a bag of salt and see if I could trade with some of the women for what he needs?" she asked.

"Take two just in case they drive a hard bargain. You're absolutely right. He can't go on like that. I just can't believe Yani hasn't noticed," said Deet

"That Yani hasn't noticed what," asked Yani as she walked up behind them.

"That Cru needs warmer clothes if he's going to make this trip without getting frozen feet," said Etta.

"And what makes you think I haven't already thought of it," she said with a smile. "I've already talked to Ana and she's spreading the word among the women. I was just coming to get Cru so we could make sure that what I trade for will fit. Etta, will you go to my pack and get several scrapers and a couple of knife blades. And maybe a bag of salt just in case they had something special I may want to trade for," she said before turning toward where Cru was playing.

"I should have known she would be one step ahead of us," said Deet with a laugh. "You better go get her trade goods and I need to get back to these waiting customers."

Cru was torn between being thrilled at the new clothes he would be getting and being impatient to get back outside so he could play. He knew his next few days would be back to the trail with no time for play. Finally, Yani finished the deal. Four of her scrapers and two knives had been enough to provide Cru with all that he needed. As they left the group of women who had gathered in front of Ana's house, she said to Cru, "You need to take your new moccasins and your parka off now. Until the snow falls, you will be carrying them in your pack. Especially the moccasins. You don't want to put any more wear on them than necessary."

Reluctantly, Cru pulled off his new winter moccasins and parka and handed them to Etta. He followed her to where they had left the packs and watched as she stowed them away.

"Don't look so glum," said Etta. "You'll be wearing them soon enough. The snow will be here before we know it. Then you'll wish for this mild weather again."

# Chapter Six

Several days after they had left the Village with the Well, as they were nearing the next village, Deet walked up beside Etta. Touching her arm he indicated she should slow her pace so they were out of earshot of Yani. Once they had fallen back a bit, Deet whispered to her. "This next village has a surprise for Yani. It's the village where her sister Kali lives. It has been many summers since they've seen each other. You may want to stay near her so you can see her reaction when she realizes where she is."

"Shouldn't we tell her before we get there?" asked Etta.

"No," replied Deet. "Let it be a surprise. She may figure it out when we get near the village. It is called the Village in the Oaks so we enter an oak forest just before we get there. But if she doesn't recognize it, let's just see what happens."

As they walked, Etta moved up so she could be walking next to Yani as they entered the village. Soon the trail left the meadow they had been crossing and entered the gloom of a mature oak forest. Yani seemed to be lost in thought as they walked. Suddenly she stopped and pointed. "Look, Etta," Yani cried in a hushed voice. "See on that branch! It's a cedar wax wing. I remember seeing one of those birds the day after I left my village the first time with the Knapper."

They stopped and watched the bird for a moment until Deet and Cru caught up to them. Hearing them approach Yani turned and indicated they should come up to her slowly and quietly. When they were close enough she pointed out the bird to them. She whispered, "I think that is an omen. I last saw one when I was on the journey south with the Knapper. I think it means something good is going to happen soon."

They stood and watched the bird until it flew off then returned to their trek. As they began walking again, Deet winked at Etta.

It was just past midday when they walked into the village. They had just rounded the first house when they heard a woman call out, "Yani! Come back here, you imp! Stop running!"

Yani stopped in her tracks and looked around puzzled. She was not running so who was this telling her to stop and why? She had just taken another few steps when a small girl with bright blonde hair barreled around the corner of the house and into her.

"Whoa there," Yani said as she caught the child. "Not so fast."

The next moment a woman came running around the house following her. "Yani I told you to stop. Why don't you…" she started saying. When she saw Yani she came to an abrupt halt. Taking a step toward her, she said, "Yani? Is it really you?"

Looking up at her mother, the child said, "Mother, of course it is me. You know that."

When her mother didn't respond, the child looked up at the woman who had her hands on her shoulders. Yani finally said, "Kali, is that you?"

Letting the child go, Yani approached Kali and wrapped her arms around her sister. The others watched as the two sisters hugged. Finally Yani held Kali at arms-length and said, "It has been far too long. Let me look at you."

"Who is that?" asked Cru as he watched.

"Well, you know your mother and Yani are sisters?" said Deet. "Well, this is Kali their other sister. So she is also your aunt."

"But why did she call this little girl Yani?" asked Cru.

"Because I am Yani," said the girl, stomping her foot for emphasis. "Don't you know anything. I am Yani, not her. She can't have my name. It's mine!"

Kneeling in front of the little girl, Yani said, "I hate to disappoint you but I have been Yani a lot longer than you have."

"That's right, daughter. This is my sister, Yani. She is who you were named after," said Kali with a big smile for her sister.

Turning to the other visitors, Kali welcomed them to the village and lead them to the village headman's house. On the way Kali asked to be introduced to the others. "I remember Deet but don't know who these two young people are."

"This is Etta, she has lived with me since she lost her parents in the big fire. And this rascal is Cru. He is Dami and Dorf's son. So Cru meet your Aunt Kali and your cousin Yani."

As the adults talked with the headman of the village, Etta removed the packs from the goats. Kali's daughter watched all of them from a distance. Once the goats were unloaded, Etta and Cru led them to a small patch of dried grass at the far end of the village. It was not big enough to be called a meadow but would provide the goats with fodder while they were here in this village. When the goats were staked, Cru and Black began to explore the area. As he had in each of the villages they had visited, he had Black on a lead. This village didn't have a herd of sheep that could be a risk from Black but Cru wanted Black to be used to being on a lead in the villages. As they wandered near the edge of the forest, young Yani followed behind him.

It didn't take long for Cru to make a circle around the village. When he found himself back where the goats were staked he sat down beside Frisky. As he ran his hand down the side of the feeding goat, he noticed some burs in her coat. He started picking them lose. As he worked to clean the goats coat, he soon became aware he was being watched. Without stopping his work he glanced at the edge of the forest After a couple of times of scanning the trees, he spotted her. "Yani, you might as well come over here and talk to me," he called. "You know, I see you hiding behind that tree."

"If I come out, will you make sure your wolf doesn't eat me?" came a small voice.

"That depends on how nice you are to me," replied Cru. "You know Black only likes nice little girls."

"Maybe I should stay here then," said Yani.

Laughing Cru said, "I was only teasing. Black is a nice wolf and doesn't eat little girls. Come here and I'll let you pet him."

Hesitantly the little girl approached Cru. She stopped a few steps away. Cru continued to pick the burs out of Frisky's coat and after a moment he said, "Come on over and sit beside Black. He likes to have his ears scratched."

Not convinced, Yani only inched forward a couple steps. "Is that one of the ugly sheep that Birg travels with?"

"Ugly sheep! That's funny. They aren't sheep. They're goats. And I don't think they are ugly. I think they're pretty. They have such soft silky coats. Come here and feel it," said Cru.

Taking a circular route around Black she came up to the goats. "Do they bite?" asked Yani.

"Once in a while but these two are really sweet and they never bite. They might nibble a little but it doesn't hurt."

Slowly Yani overcame her fear and reached out and touched the one Cru had named Steady on her head. "Oh, it is so soft," she cried.

"That's what I told you. The long hair on her side is even softer. Come around beside me and you can help me pick out the burs. I'm not sure where they picked up these burs but we need to get them out. When they have their packs on they would really hurt."

Yani cautiously joined Cru and after watching a few moments started working the burs loose from the long silk hair. By the time they had all the burs removed from the goats it was late in the afternoon. Standing, Cru said, "I think I need to go see if Yani or Deet needs me. Do you want to come along?"

"She is not Yani! I'm Yani!" yelled the little girl. Hearing the anger in her voice, Black growled softly. The growl stopped the tantrum. "Don't let your wolf eat me," whispered Yani.

"Black is not going to eat you. But when he hears someone yelling angrily he gets upset. Now listen. For the last time, you are both Yani. I'm going to call you Little Yani. Then you will know you are different."

"Why don't you call her Big Yani? Why do I have to be different?" she insisted.

"I think I will do both. You are Little Yani and Yani is Big Yani. How's that?" asked Cru.

After thinking for a bit Little Yani said, "I guess that will be alright."

"There they are," said Etta when the two children walked around the house with Black between them. "I was wondering where you were."

"Little Yani was helping me pick the burs out of Frisky and Steady's coats. She was a big help," said Cru.

"And you need to call me Little Yani and that other woman is Big Yani. That way you don't get us confused," said the girl.

"What a good idea," replied Etta. "Little Yani it is. I was looking for you because it is time to eat. Kali has supper ready. So come on you two."

They spent the night in the Village in the Oaks and the next day while Yani and Kali visited, Deet did some trading. Etta and Cru enjoyed the day of rest. They knew the next day they would be back on the trail again.

When morning came, after a tearful farewell between the sisters, the travelers resumed their journey.

# Chapter Seven

The weather held as they continued their journey toward the mountains far to the south. The trading had been good. They had visited several villages that were new to Yani. Each time they came to a new village she would seek out the medicine woman to share knowledge and trade herbs. Most of the time they both used the same plants but occasionally she would learn of a new plant. Usually, it was a plant that did not grow in her area, like the plants she had learned about from Gyla. She often thought of Gyla, the wise woman who had taught her about medicine plants in the village she and the Knapper had summered in on that long ago trip to the Mountains That Are Always White.

A moon later they had finished trading in a village at the base of a range of mountains that had a coat of new winter snow. Since they had finished their trading, they were preparing to move on the next day. They were sharing a final meal with Wout, the headman of the village, when he asked, " Are you planning on using the pass over the mountain or taking the long way around and down the river?"

"I was thinking we would go over the pass," answered Deet. "I know we will be in some snow but it doesn't look like much snow on the trail through the pass. It seems to be just higher up on the slopes."

"Yes, the trail should be clear. The danger now is avalanche. We had a deep snow up there a moon ago then the weather turned warm for a few days followed by another snow. When that happens – a snow followed by a warm spell and then more snow – the snow becomes unstable. With these conditions it may not be safe to go over the pass," explained the headman.

"So you think it would not be safe to go through the pass? It's much shorter than the river trail," said Deet.

"I can't say. You may be fine or you may be buried in a mountain of snow. I just wanted you to be aware of the possibility of danger. Personally, I would go the long way along the river. Have you ever seen an avalanche?" asked Wout.

"No," replied Deet.

"Have you?" asked Wout turning to Yani.

"No," she replied. "This is only my second time to make this trip. I have little experience with these mountains. And know nothing of, what did you call it, an avalanche?"

"Then let me tell you about avalanches. When the snow is unstable anything can set it off. A loud noise. A strong wind. Or just the weight of the snow. At first it looks like the snow is trembling. Then the top layer of snow begins sliding down hill. By the time you realize what is happing a whole mountain side of snow is ripping downslope at you. If it reaches you, the snow will bury you. The weight of the snow makes it impossible for you to move."

"What are the chances of an avalanche?" asked Etta.

"There is no way to tell. It may not happen at all this winter. Or there could be several."

"We will have to think it over. We have a half day's walk until we get to where the trail forks. We can make up our minds on the way," said Deet.

"I wish you a safe journey then," said Wout. "But if I were you I would take the river trail."

The next morning, they were on the trail as the sun turned the snow on the mountain to a delicate pink. As they walked Yani and Deet discussed whether they should go over the mountain or around.

"If we go on the river trail how many more days will it take us than going over the pass?" asked Yani as she walked beside Deet.

"I have only taken that trail once and it was many summers ago. If I remember correctly it took me ten days. But I was young and strong then and moved more quickly. If we take the river trail, I think we should plan on it taking at least fifteen days," he replied.

"That's half a moon. Such a long time," said Yani. "I think we should try the pass. If it looks dangerous when we start up, we can always turn around and come back. The river trail will still be there."

They walked in silence for a while thinking. Then Deet said, "The pass is it. I have been looking at the snow and it looks like any other snow I've seen. Maybe Wout was just being overly cautious."

The sun was high in the sky when they reached the fork in the trail. They stopped for a rest and to eat a little before starting the climb. There was a spring nearby so they filled their water gourds. They knew they could always melt the snow to drink but it would mean making a fire and they didn't want to delay that long in the crossing.

As they started up the slope into the pass the animals stayed unusually close to the travelers. The goats who usually frisked ahead of them seemed hesitant to go forward. Black and Wolf stayed by the sides of Cru and Yani. They were just nearing the edge of the snow field when Wolf stopped in the trail. He growled softly. Kneeling by him Yani asked, "What's the problem, Wolf? Is there someone or something up ahead that you don't like the smell of."

As Yani reassured Wolf, the goats moved back down the trail until they were behind the others. Black was also reluctant to move on. Looking at their four-legged friends, Deet said, "Maybe I need to go up the trail a ways and see it there is someone there."

"No," cried Cru. "I think we all need to run back down the trail. And run very fast! Look! The snow is moving."

When the others looked where he was pointing, they saw the snow beginning to ripple and shift. Before they could respond the mountainside began to slip toward them. Horrified, they turned and ran. Wolf nipped at Black as he started up the trail to attack the oncoming danger turning him to follow the others. They all ran head long down the trail with the sound of the oncoming mountain of snow following them.

"See those big boulders ahead at the side of the trail?' called Deet. "Try to get behind them before the snow catches up with us. Run!"

Etta was the first to reach the boulders and quickly ducked behind them. Just as she did Cru ran past. She reached out and grabbed him and pulled him to the shelter of the rocks. He was trembling all over and looked up at her with terror filled eyes. "Are we going to die?" he asked.

"Not if I can help it," said Etta as she pushed him further into the shelter of the boulders.

Yani and Wolf staggered into the shelter just as the first wave of snow rumbled past them covering the trail. They pushed back farther into the protection of the huge rocks when Yani looked around. "Where's Deet?" she cried. Etta was just able to stop her from diving into the river of snow.

'Yani, stop! We can't help Deet if we get trapped in the snow, too. Yani!" Etta cried, holding tightly to the struggling woman.

"I know," sobbed Yani, "but we have to find him."

"We will, but not until it stops," she replied.

"Where are the goats?" asked Cru. "Wolf and Black are here but the goats are gone."

"We can worry about the goats later. But first Deet," said Etta.

As suddenly as it started the avalanche stopped. The silence after the thunderous noise was frightening. It took a moment for them to realize it was over then Etta flew into action. "Wolf, find Deet," she ordered as she move out over the snow. Wolf followed by Black, leaped into action searching over the river of snow for a scent of the man. Yani and Etta clamored behind them looking for any sign of their friend. Cru struggled after them, digging at anything that might be Deet. Wolf's frantic barking drew them to where he had begun to dig. As soon as Etta reached Wolf she dropped to her knees and scraped at the snow. Yani, Cru and Black soon joined them.

"How can snow that was moving minutes ago be so hard and packed?" asked Cru.

"Keep digging," replied Yani. "He must be here. We have to reach him."

It seemed they had been digging forever when Black grabbed something and began to pull. "He's here," cried Yani. "Black found him. He has a hold on his arm. Good boy, Black. Now keep digging."

They all concentrated on the area around the arm that was protruding for the snow. Soon Yani was able to clear the snow from around his head. "Deet, look at me. Can you hear me?" pleaded Yani.

Blinking the snow from his eyes Deet nodded slightly.

"He's alive!" cried Yani. "Dig! Quickly!"

Moving out from his head they all kept digging until they uncovered enough of him to see the way his body was laying under the snow. Once they had an idea where they should concentrate the digging they worked frantically. After what seemed like a lifetime, they had him freed.

"Deet, can you move?" asked Etta leaning over him.

"I don't know," answered Deet in a whisper. "It hurts to breathe."

"We need to get you back down the trail to where we can build a fire and get you warm. Can you try to sit up?" asked Yani.

Reaching behind him Yani gently supported his back as he attempted to sit up. Once he had made it to a sitting position Yani supported him as he winced with pain. "I think I have a broken rib," Deet muttered.

"Let me feel," said Yani as she slid her hands up under Deet's parka. She gently ran her hands along both of his sides and was relieved to find no jagged edges indicating a badly broken rib. If they are just cracked there was little danger of puncturing the lungs as could happen if they were broken and out of place.

"They feel like they are just cracked. You need to move now. If we don't get you warmed up soon you could freeze. Now you have to try to stand up," ordered Yani.

Deet groaned and after a weak effort fell back. "I can't," he said.

"Yes, you can! And you will," yelled Yani. "Now stop this silliness and get on your feet. If not, I am going to take these children down the trail and leave you here to freeze. Now up!" With that Yani grabbed him under the arms and pulled with all her might. Deet cried out but managed to get to his feet. Calling over her shoulder to Etta and Cru, she said, "You two bring the packs. We have to get him to a fire."

Yani stumbled ahead through the snow with Deet's arm draped over her shoulder. Each step they took Deet groaned but he kept going. It was difficult at first but before too long the snow began to thin out and then they were walking on bare trail. Once they were out of the snow Yani looked for a clear place they could stop and start a fire. She had just settled Deet in a good spot when Etta and Cru caught up with them. Dropping the two packs she was carrying Etta said to Yani. "I need to go back and get Deet's pack, it's still buried in the snow. Can you manage without me?"

"No, you stay here. That pack is not going anywhere and you are exhausted. Help me get a fire going then find a pot in my pack and get some water. I hear a stream over that way. Cru hurry and gather some wood. I'll look for the acorn meal. We all need something warm."

Pulling a sleeping cloak out of her pack she wrapped it around Deet. "I wish we had some of those seal skin clothes that the Seapeople wear. You wouldn't be nearly so cold. As soon as I get a fire going, we'll warm you up." Yani said as she wrapped her arms around the shivering man.

"I'm sorry, Yani," Deet whispered.

"And just what are you sorry for?" asked Yani. "Unless you mean for being a big baby back there and making me yell at you." Yani chuckled and she held him in her arms.

"I should have taken the river trail. I should have listened to the advice we got in the last village. Now we have lost the goats with most of our trade goods and maybe my pack. I have broken ribs. We may not be able to go any farther and it is all my fault."

"As I remember we both agreed that it was worth the risk to take the pass. It was not just your idea. As far as the goats go, I am quite sure they will turn up. Your ribs will heal and if we lose your pack, it will not be the end of the world. Now I have to get a fire started." Giving him a kiss on the cheek she joined Cru at the fire pit he had scraped into the dirt.

# Chapter Eight

Back in the village, Wout stood looking at the mountain range. He was very uneasy about the traders. The snow had looked unstable for the last few days and he was afraid they would be foolish and take the quicker route over the pass. He had just begun to turn back to his house when he saw the snow begin to move.

"I hope they took the river trail," he muttered as he entered his house. He had settled by his fire and continued adding a new point to his spear but his mind kept going to the travelers. He got up and put another log on the fire when he heard a commotion outside. Looking out he saw some of the village boys trying to catch the goats of the traders. Seeing the terrified goats, he feared the travelers had been caught in an avalanche. Calling to the boys, he said, "Leave the goats alone and run to get your fathers. We need to see if our friends have been caught by the avalanche. Hurry now."

As the boys scattered to spread the word, Wout returned to his house to collect the warm bear hides they used when travelers were caught in the sudden snowstorms that roared down the pass in the winter. By the time he had returned to the commons, the men of the village had gathered with digging tools and more furs.

The goats followed as the men jogged down the trail toward the base of the pass. As the sun dropped low in the sky, they spotted the smoke from the fire. Slowing the pace a bit, Wout said to his companions, "At least some of them escaped the avalanche. With luck they will all have made it out of the pass safely."

Cru had just walked out of the woods back into the clearing with an arm load of firewood when one of the goats trotted into the camp. Seeing it he dropped his load of firewood and ran to it. Dropping to his knees he wrapped his arms around the goat's neck and murmured into its soft fur, "Oh, Frisky, you didn't die. I thought the avalanche had buried you. But where is Steady?"

"Frisky and Steady?" asked Etta. 'When did you come up with those names?"

"I named them as we walked along. Frisky was always skipping ahead and up over things and Steady just walked along calmly. You know, nice and steady. But where is Steady? Do you think the snow got him?" asked a teary-eyed Cru.

"No, I think he is just walking nice and steady with our rescuers. Look," said Etta pointing up the trail.

Wout and his fellow villagers came into sight loaded down with the things they would need to help the travelers. As he entered the clearing Wout said, "I'm relieved to see you all are safe. I was afraid you had taken the pass."

"You are half right. We are safe but we had started up the pass. Luckily, we are much slower than we used to be. We had just started to climb when the snow let go. With exception of Deet we had all managed to get to the big boulders along the trail before the snow caught us. Unfortunately, he was buried. Wolf and Black were able to find him in time. But he has a couple cracked ribs and he lost his pack. The pack's not a problem but I am afraid we may need to take advantage of your hospitality for a few days more as he heals enough to move on."

"We would be honored," replied Wout. "But first let's get him warm." With that he wrapped Deet in one of the bear skins he had brought.

Wout who had rescued travelers from avalanches before insisted they spend the night where they were. They had a nice fire, plenty of wood available and water nearby. He knew from experience that the shock of the near miss would hit them soon. The best thing would be to make sure they were well fed and wrapped up warm. As he fed the fire once more before going to sleep himself, he made sure they were all wrapped securely in the bear skins they had brought. Once he was sure they were all nice and snug he rolled in his sleeping cloak and slept.

The next morning Wout was awake before the rest. As his fellow villagers awoke, he motioned for them to come away from the sleeping travelers. Once they were out of earshot he said quietly, "We need to get them back to the village as soon as we can but I'm not sure Deet can walk that far. If we make a sling out of one of the bear skins, do you think you can carry him?" he directed this to Liam and Cam, the two youngest and strongest. When they nodded, he turned to Ott. "Do you think you can go back where the snow caught them and see if you can find Deet's pack. If it is buried too deep don't worry about it. But I think we should try. You should be able to find where they dug him out. If it is not there it will be buried until the thaw next spring." Ott just nodded and started jogging up the trail toward the pass.

Back by the campfire Etta was stirring. She quietly got up and taking a cooking pot went to the stream to get water to heat. She wanted to have warm food ready when the others woke up. Seeing Wout she walked over to greet him. "Thank you again for coming to our rescue. The bear skin was wonderful. I think I would have shivered all night without it. As it was it took a while before I warmed up. And I wasn't even buried in the snow like Deet."

"It happens often after a narrow escape with an avalanche. I don't know why but I've seen it many times. We keep the bear skins handy for just that."

"Again, thank you. I'm going to get some water so I can make some porridge. The others will need something warm to eat when they wake up," giving Wout a warm smile Etta headed for the stream.

Etta had the porridge bubbling by the fire when Yani woke. Staying wrapped in the warm bear skin, she said, "I see you have a good breakfast ready for us. But I think I'll just enjoy this nice warm cocoon I'm in for a little bit longer."

"That's a good idea. Would you like me to bring some porridge over to you? That way you can stay warm and fill your tummy at the same time."

"Yes, please, that sounds wonderful," smiled Yani.

Etta filled a bowl with the steaming porridge, then carried it over to Yani. Sitting beside her Etta whispered, "We were very lucky yesterday, weren't we?"

"Yes, we were indeed very lucky. We could all have been killed. I don't know if I have ever been that close to crossing over to the Otherside. Without Cru's sharp eyes I don't think we would have made it. He saw the avalanche starting and warned us just in time. And without Wolf and Black I think we would have lost Deet. I go all cold inside just thinking of it." Yani shivered.

"But we didn't get killed and we found Deet in time. That's the important thing," said Etta. "It turns out it was a good thing we let Cru come after all." Looking over to where the boy slept, she smiled at Yani.

They sat quietly as Yani ate her porridge. When she finished, Etta said, "Why don't you go back to sleep a while longer. I'll wake you when Deet wakes up. For now, sleep is good for all three of you."

"And what about you?" asked Yani.

"I may lie down for a bit myself," Etta replied as she settled the bear skin back around Yani and took her bowl.

As Yani, Deet and Cru slept, Etta looked through her pack for one of the pouches of the fat and dried berries the Seapeople had given her on their last visit. She was sure Deet would need it when he woke up. She just hoped Yani was right about his ribs just being cracked. Once she found what she was looking for, she too curled up in a bear skin to sleep a while more.

The sun had climbed high into the sky and was warming the campsite when Etta woke up again. Wout had kept the fire going as they slept. Joining him next to the blaze she asked, "Where are the rest of our rescuers? Did they decide we were going to sleep forever?"

"No, they just decided to make themselves useful," replied Wout with a smile. "Ott went back to the avalanche to see if he could find Deet's pack and..."

"Deet's pack!" cried Etta, "I was going to go after it first thing this morning."

"Not to worry," said Wout. "If it can be found Ott will find it. And your black wolf went with him. Between the two of them I think they will find it. You need to rest."

"And Liam and Cam?"

"They went a little way up the trail to cut two stout trees to make a sling so they could carry Deet back to the village. I am pretty sure he won't be able to walk it on his own."

"He's not going to like that but you're right. Yani may have to yell at him again," said Etta as she giggled. "When Deet was having trouble getting up after we dug him out, Yani had to yell at him to get him moving. I think that's the first time I have ever heard her yell at anyone. And it worked. She got him to his feet."

Hearing their hushed voices Yani woke. Rising she joined them at the fire. "Is there any more of that porridge left," she asked Etta. "For some reason I am starving."

Etta filled a bowl of the porridge for Yani then sat down beside her. "Before you start on the porridge why don't you eat a little of this." She said handing the pouch of fat and berries to her.

Taking it Yani smiled and said, "You're right. I should have thought of it yesterday as soon as we made camp." Scooping a healthy gob out of the bag she popped it in her mouth. After swallowing she began to lick the excess off her fingers.

Watching her with interest Wout asked, "What is that?"

"Here," said Etta, taking the pouch from Yani and handing it to Wout. "Try it. It is fat from seals and whales mixed with dried berries. We trade with the Seapeople for it. When it is cold it seems to help you stay warm. We carry several pouches with us for emergencies."

Wout cautiously smelled the contents. "Phew, it smells like old fish. You eat this stuff?"

Laughing Yani said, "It is an acquired taste but truly the taste is not bad. Be brave and try it."

Using a finger Wout scooped out a tiny bit of the thick gray mixture and licked it off. As the fat melted in the warmth of his mouth the look on his face changed. "You're right it does taste better than it smells. But tell me again what it is. I've never heard of either of those animals."

"Then you're in for a treat when we get Deet back to your village. He's a fine storyteller. A few summers ago, he decided at the end of the summer to go with the Seapeople on their boats so he could go to the ice to hunt seal. And Etta can tell you all about whales too. While we wait for Deet to heal we'll earn our food and shelter with stories."

"You might have asked me before you set me up as a storyteller" mumbled Deet from the bear skin he was wrapped in.

"He's the best storyteller ever," cried Cru as he popped up from his nest of furs. "I love the story of the seal hunt. He saw Northern Lights and big white bears and…"

"Enough, Boy, you'll give away all the exciting parts," said Deet as he slowly sat up.

"Is that porridge I smell?" asked Cru as he crawled out of the covers.

# Chapter Nine

As they were preparing to leave the campsite Ott showed up with Deet's pack. Dropping it next to the cold firepit, he said, "It wasn't hard to find. Actually, it was less than an arm's length from where you had dug Deet out of the snow. I had to dig a little but it was really this guy who found it." As he finished talking, he patted Black on the head.

"Thank you, Ott," said Deet. "I've carried that pack since I was twelve summers. I would have hated to lose it. We could have managed without the goods I have in it but that pack means a lot to me,"

"And I thank you, too," said Etta with a big smile. "If you hadn't gone back, I would have had to."

"I was glad to help," replied Ott with a shy smile.

The trip back to the village was a slow painful trip for Deet. He had objected to being carried at first but after walking a few steps he gave in and lower himself into the bear skin stretched between the poles Liam and Cam had cut. The distance that had taken them only part of a day on the outward trip seemed to go on forever on the return. As a result, it was long after dark when they finally neared the village. Cru was so tired by then he was having trouble staying on his feet. Finally, Etta picked him up. Smiling at her, he mumbled, "Thank you. I think I was…" And with that he fell asleep on her shoulder.

When they entered the village Wout pointed Etta and Cru to his house and then took Yani and Deet to see the medicine woman. As soon as they entered her house Deet dropped down on the sleeping bench by the fire. Before he had a chance to lie down, Rosa, the medicine woman, stopped him.

"Before I let you sleep, I need to check your injuries." Turning to Yani she said, "I know you've examined him but with your permission I would like to see for myself."

"Of, course," said Yani. "It's always good to have two opinions. Deet, let me help you take your parka off so Rosa can see your ribs."

"Do I have a say in this?" asked Deet. "You know they are my ribs."

"No, in this case you do not. Now be a good patient and do as you're told," replied Yani gently caressing his check. Then she eased his parka off exposing his badly bruised ribs.

"Oh, my, that looks very painful," said Rosa.

"And it feels even worse than it looks," groaned Deet.

"I think we should apply a poultice and then wrap him so he doesn't dislocate the breaks," said Rosa.

"I agree," replied Yani. "I have some herbs that might be just the things for the poultice."

As Yani rummaged through her pack for the herbs she had in mind, Rosa stirred up the fire to heat some water. As the two women went about their work, Deet laid back on the bench and was soon asleep.

Several nights later as the travelers were gathered around the fire in Wout's house, Cru said, "Deet, you haven't told them about the seal hunt yet. Have you forgotten you promised?"

"Actually, I'm not sure I remember anything about telling stories but if you think these friends would like to hear that old boring tale, I might be persuaded to give it a try," replied Deet with a twinkle in his eye.

"But it's not boring. It's one of the best stories ever. You would love to hear it, wouldn't you, Wout?" pleaded Cru.

"Well, I must admit I am a little curious about these animals that live on the ice way up north. That is if you feel up to it Deet," replied Wout.

"I'm sure he does, don't you, Deet? That's my favorite story that he tells," cried Cru.

"Well, alright but maybe you should go and get Liam and Cam since they were interested in hearing it, too," said Deet.

As Cru ducked out the door in search of the two young men, Yani grinned at Deet. "You know you really shouldn't tease him like that. You love telling that story and I happen to know you have just been waiting for the chance to tell it."

"You're right on both counts. But it's so much fun to tease Cru. And I didn't string him along very long this time," chuckled Deet.

"They're coming," cried Cru as he scrambled through the door and back to his spot by the fire next to Black. Liam and Cam followed him in and were soon settled on one of the sleeping benches.

Clearing his throat and looking around at his audience, Deet transformed into his storyteller mode. In his deep sing-song voice he started, "Five summers ago I journeyed with the Seapeople in their boats across the Northern Sea to their home in the cold Northlands. For seven long days and seven dark nights we were out of sight of land."

"And the number of days and nights increase with each telling," whispered Yani.

"As I said, we were out of sight of land for an exceptionally long time. The waves rocked the boat and splashed the water over the sides but the Seapeople only laughed at the hostile sea. At last, we sighted a faint line on the horizon and soon we approached the Northland. The Seapeople dropped the sail that had been catching the wind and pushing us forward. Once the sail was lowered and rolled up the men grabbed long paddles and began to row toward the shore. When they came to a river, they rowed the boat upstream and soon came to a sheltered spot where they moored the boat.

"The men unloaded their cargo and we walked the short distance from the river to the village. It was very much like ours, only they had a strange way of building their houses. First they dig holes in the ground and build the houses over these holes. You had to walk down several steps just to enter. It turned out that this kept the houses warmer in winter and cooler in summer. And their winters are much colder and longer than ours so they needed that extra warmth."

"They built me a house in that style when I moved from the beach to the top of the cliff after the big wave. But that is another story. Go ahead, Deet. I'm sorry I interrupted," said Yani.

"Thank you," said Deet, "anyway before I was interrupted, I was saying. What was I saying?"

"The houses were sunk in holes to keep them warmer," said Cru.

"Thank you, Cru. As soon as the weather was cold enough the men of the village prepared for the seal hunt. This time we traveled in smaller boats and stayed close to the shore. At the end of the day, we had gone as far as we could. The way ahead was blocked by ice. We pulled the boats up on to the rocky shore and unloaded the supplies we had brought. There was a small house here for us to sleep in and several storage buildings. Once we had everything unloaded and stowed away, we gathered in the sleeping hut and settled for the night. The next morning before the sun was even up, we started out onto the ice for the hunt. In the storage buildings were several sleds. We loaded them with harpoons - spear-like weapons that had a very large hook like you would use to catch fish only bigger and a line attached. It was still dark when we started out onto the ice because the days are noticeably shorter there in the wintertime. Olf, he is the headman of the village I visited, told me that in the middle of winter as far north as we were, there were days the sun never came above the horizon and in the summer it never set. I am not sure if that is true but can tell you that on that day the sun came up extremely late and did not rise more than halfway up into the sky.

"As we made our way across the ice the men broke away in pairs to look for a blow hole. Seals live in the sea but they are not fish so they must breathe. They keep holes in the ice open so they can crawl out on the ice to breathe. I went with Olf.. We soon found a hole and settle down to wait. It wasn't long before bubbles appeared in the water. I watched as a gray head popped up followed by a sleek body. Olf was positioned next to the hole, so as soon as the seal lunged out for some air, he drove the harpoon deep into its body just behind its head. With my help, we pulled the seal from the hole and across the ice away from any possible escape. As soon as we had it clear of the hole, Olf thanked the gods and the spirit of the animal and killed it. We loaded it on the sled then it was my turn to try. I knelt by the hole to wait. I was about ready to give up when the bubbles appeared. But I was too anxious and threw the harpoon too soon hitting the seal in the head instead of the body. My harpoon skidded off the hard skull and the seal disappeared into the water. I was upset by my mistake but Olf explained that it was a common mistake. We settled back to wait some more and the next time a seal appeared I was successful. Olf took the position at the hole again and soon we had three fat seals on the sled. Seeing that the sun had started to dip low in the sky we started the long slow trek back across the ice. It was much slower on the return trip because our sled was weighted down with our catch. Let me tell you what a seal looks like. Let's see, seals are about the same size as Wolf here. Their fur is amazingly sleek and soft. One of the best things is it repels water so if you have a seal skin parka on and are caught in a storm, you stay dry. And they have a thick layer of fat under their skin. They don't have legs instead they have flippers that they use to swim. All in all, they are very strange looking animals. Here let me show you." Picking us a stick from the pile of kindle by the fire, Deet scratched the shape of a seal in the dirt of the floor.

"But back to the hunt and our return to the huts. The stars had just begun to appear in the sky when something large and heavy crashed into me knocking me to the ground. I turned over quickly to find myself staring into the maw of a huge white bear. I was helpless against it since I had put my spear and harpoon on the sled so it was easier for me to pull. Luckily for me Olf began yelling and waving his arms to distract it. Not so lucky for Olf as the bear turned and attacked him. Olf had grabbed his spear when the bear jumped me so he was armed at least. As soon as the bear turned toward him, he threw it. Unfortunately, with its big front paw, the bear knocked the spear away before using the opposite paw to swat Olf knocking him down. Before it could finish its attack on Olf I was able to drive my spear into its back. Feeling the blade bury into its body it turned on me. Olf had gained his feet by then and he too drove his spear into the bear. As it fell forward onto me again Olf climbed on its back and slit its throat. With Olf's help I was able to climb out from under the beast. As soon as we caught our breath, we skinned it, stowed the bear skin on the sled and headed back toward camp. Banged up and tired we only wanted to get to camp and go to bed.

"And speaking of bed, it's time for Cru to head for his bed. He needs to rest because I think tomorrow, we can start on our way again."

"Do I have…" started Cru.

"Yes, you do," replied Yani. "We all need to get rested. So off you go."

'Come on, Cru," said Etta. "I'll join you."

The young people crawled onto their sleeping bench leaving Yani, Deet and Wout sitting around the fire. As soon as Cru's breathing told them that he was sound asleep Deet continued his story for Wout.

"I don't like to tell this part in front of the boy. As it turns out Olf and I both were injured pretty badly by the bear. Its claws, which are bigger that any I have ever seen, cut through my parka and tore a deep gash into my shoulder and arm. Olf had several cracked ribs. We may not have made it back to camp if Sven and Jorg hadn't come looking for us. Olf and I were too banged up to go back out on the ice the next day. The others went out once more but, because of our injuries, we had to end the hunt early. By the time we reached Olf's village I was very sick. The wounds from the bear's claws had festered. As soon as we got back to the village they took me to Ana, the medicine woman in the next village, and I spent the winter recovering at her house. The wound had become so badly infected that only her wise care had saved me. As it is I still carry some impressive scars.

"And now I think it is time that I too get some sleep. Are you ready, Yani?"

Together they left Wout's house and made their way to their beds.

# Chapter Ten

The next morning the travelers were again making their way south. This time when they reached the split in the trail they turned and followed the river. They skirted the mountains along a trail that led through a pine forest where the land began its upward tilt. The path was broad and flat making travel easy. As they walked the goats munched on any plants they discovered along the way. Black wandered off in search of game while Wolf walked by Yani matching her pace. The day was mild making the journey pleasant. When the sun began to dip low, they began looking for a good place to camp for the night. They soon found a small clearing near a brook that trickled out of the hillside and began to settle for the night.

They each knew their assigned tasks. Cru collected firewood. Etta filled the cooking pot with water. Yani got the acorn meal out of her pack after unloading the goats. Deet walked a short distance away looking for any squirrel that might be in the trees. With luck they would have some fresh meat in their porridge.

Soon Etta had a fire burning in the fire pit she had made. As Deet walked out of the woods with two fat squirrels, Black also appear with a rabbit in his jaws. As they watched, Black carried the rabbit to Wolf and dropped it by him. As soon as he dropped the rabbit he looked around as if to say, "Now aren't I a good boy?" Wolf sniffed at the rabbit then picked it up and carried it to Yani. Patting him she gave it back to him saying, "No, Wolf, Black brought this for you. We have our squirrels, You and Black can share the rabbit." Walking over to Black, Yani dropped to her knees and hugged him. "Thank you, Black. I am happy to see you taking care of Wolf. I think his hunting days may be numbered."

It didn't take long for them to have a warm supper ready. Once they had eaten, they curled up in their sleeping cloaks and settled down for the night. Soon the travelers were sleeping, all except Wolf. He kept a watchful eye on the thicket at the edge of the trail they were to travel the next morning. His instincts told him there was danger ahead.


After a good night's sleep, the travelers continued their journey. As they followed the path, Wolf kept a watchful eye on the forest around him. He could not identify what was disturbing him but he knew something was not right. No one else seemed to sense danger but he was sure they were not safe. Several times during the day he wandered off the trail into the woods but soon returned having found nothing amiss.

They paused to eat and rest when the sun was directly overhead. As they ate their jerky, the goats kept close to them rather than wandering off to browse. Wolf kept his watchful vigilance rather than falling asleep as usual. Even Black was not at ease.

"Deet, I think something's not right. The animals aren't acting normal. But I can't see anything that could be upsetting them. Do you have any ideas?" asked Yani.

"I've noticed that too," he replied.

"So have I," said Etta. "And I keep feeling like someone or something is following us."

"Until we figure it out, we all stay close together. Is that understood?" said Deet looking at Cru.

"I'm not going to wander off. I promise. I feel it too," replied Cru, scooting closer to Etta.

"Good," said Deet. "I don't want you going off on a mission to be the hero and save us from who knows what. You'll walk beside Etta until we figure this out."

"I'm Etta's shadow. See," he replied as he moved even closer to her side.

"You don't have to stay quite that close," said Etta. "Just close enough that I can grab you." With that Etta grabbed him, swung him into the air, and whirled him around.

"Okay, okay, I get it," giggled Cru as she set him down.

For three days they followed the trail through the pines. What should have been a pleasant walk was marred by the ever-present feeling of being watched. The usually rambunctious Cru didn't have to be reminded to stay close to Etta. Even the animals sensed the danger. The goats limited their browsing to what grew along the trail rather than wandering off in search of weeds and grass. Wolf stayed close to Yani and Black didn't wander off in search of game as usual.

As the sun dipped low on the third day the path converged on the river they meant to follow. The pine gave way to oak and beech with thickets and berry brambles scattered throughout. The roar of the river had been steadily increasing as they neared it and now as the path began to follow it the sound made it difficult to hear each other. When they came to a wide place in the trail providing enough room for a comfortable camp, they stopped for the night. As Deet unpacked the goats, Etta and Cru walked into the woods to look for firewood.

Yani had the sleeping cloaks unpacked and water ready to heat on the fire when she realized Etta and Cru were still not back from gathering wood. "Deet, I'm going to go look for the children. They've been gone much too long. I'm sure they've just found something to distract them but still..." said Yani.

"Do you want me to go?" asked Deet. "If they've gotten into trouble, they might need me."

"No, you rest. You're still not recovered from your encounter with the avalanche. I'll find them and be back soon."

Deet smiled weakly and sank down to the ground. Yani had no doubt he would be asleep when she got back with the children. Signaling Wolf to follow her but Black to stay with Deet she started off into the woods. Wolf was more alert than usual so she pulled her sling out of the pouch she had tied to her belt. Patting Wolf she said, "Find Etta." Wolf looked at her and whined, then nose to the ground, began searching.

Etta and Cru had filled their arms with branches and were starting back to camp when suddenly Etta was jerked off her feet and found herself hanging upside down in a small clearing. Cru's first reaction was to laugh. Seconds later he realized it was a snare and began trying to release her. "Run for help, Cru. You can't get me down. Go get Deet!" cried Etta. He paused a moment then turned to dash back toward camp. He had only gone a few steps when two strong arms grabbed him.

"Not so fast there. You're not going anywhere," said his captor. "Help me tie him up, Ren."

A second man stepped out of the woods and asked, "What about her?"

"She isn't going anyplace. Now help me with this one."

They soon had Cru's hands tied when a voice said, "Let them go, Rud. I told you that if you harassed any more travelers, I would stop giving you blades. Now cut her down and turn them loose."

"Do you think that threat will work anymore? Don't you recognize who the woman with them is? We won't need your blades if we capture the knapper woman."

"And do you think she will make blades for you just because you ask?"

"No, but if she doesn't, there are lots of things I can do to these two to change her mind," replied Rud.

"And what of the man with her? Do you think he's just going to give her up without a fight?"

"He's not going to be a problem. We've been watching them and he's as weak as a baby. He's probably back in their camp asleep right now. He won't be any trouble."

"That's what you think," called Etta. "Deet will save us."

"And so will Yani," cried Cru. "You better let us go."

Wolf growled softly as they neared a clearing. Yani walked silently forward until she heard two men's voices. She stopped and listened. As she listened, she heard Etta and Cru. They sounded frightened. Taking three round stones from her pouch, she placed two in her mouth and the other in the patch of her sling. She eased forward until she had a good view of the clearing. One of the men had a firm grip on Cru. A second man was attempting to tie Etta's hands as she dangled from a rope snare. She heard a third man but he was out of site behind a bramble. Whirling the sling around several times she let fly and the stone hit the man holding Cru in the side of the head.

"Ouch! What was that?" he yelled losing his grip on Cru. As soon as he was free Cru scurried out of reach. An instant after Yani had let fly with the first stone, she had a second in her sling and ready to throw. This time she hit him between the eyes and he collapsed into a heap on the ground.

The man trying to tie up Etta stopped what he was doing and looked around to see what had attached his friend. As he turned toward Yani she let fly with another stone catching him between the eyes and knocking him unconscious, too. As she stepped into the clearing, she said to the third man who was just out of sight. "Show yourself."

Stepping into the clearing the third man dropped his spear. "I'm a friend, not a foe. I was trying to free your children from these two."

"That's right, Yani," said Etta from where she dangled from the rope. "Now if you don't mind, can you get me down. Then we can deal with those two."

As they released Etta, Cru kept watch over the two unconscious men. When they had Etta released and Cru untied Yani looked at the third man and asked, "Don't I know you?"

"Yes, Teacher, you do," he replied.

"Of course, I should have recognized those two but I had hoped they had met their end by now. Why are you still with them? I would have thought you could have broken away from them by now."

"They probably would have met their end  if I hadn't helped keep them alive. Something I'm not sure I should have done now," he replied. "So, your name is Yani. I often wondered as I thought of you. You saved my life you know. I would have starved to death long ago if you hadn't taught me to make blades so I could hunt. I have improved and make decent blades now but not as good as what you make. Again, I thank you for your kindness."

"You are welcome. And I am glad to see that you are still alive but what are we going to do with these two?" she asked.

"I think we should tie them to a tree and leave them," said Cru. "They are mean men."

"You are right there," said Etta as she pulled down the snare rope. "We have plenty of rope here for the job."

"We can't just tie them up and leave them. They would starve," protested Yani.

"No, but we could tie them up then put a knife blade near enough that if they work together they could get it and eventually get loose. And by then we would be a long way down the trail," said Cru hopefully.

"Not only are they mean men but look at their faces. They are outlaws, too. By right we should have killed them anyway," said Etta.

"You're right they are outlaws but so is your would-be rescuer. Should we kill him, too?" asked Yani.

"Well, no, he's an outlaw but he's a good man. He tried to help us," said Cru.

"You know, he has a point. We don't want them to follow us so if we tie them so it takes them a long time to get loose, we could out pace them," said Etta holding the rope.

"I say tie them up and leave them. They've been a thorn in my side long enough. They got me banished from my home and ruined my life. Give me that rope," said the third man.

'Let me help," said Etta.

By the time they had them tied to the tree, the outlaws we starting to come around. Realizing their situation, Rud began to whine. "What are you doing? You can't leave us here like this. We will die."

"Not if you work together. See we're leaving a knife here," said Yani as she laid one of her blades on the ground just out of their reach. "If you work together in a day or so you should figure out how to reach that knife and cut yourself loose. If not, then you're not meant to live. The gods will decide."

As she turned to head back to camp, Etta stopped her. "Just a moment." Turning to the third man, she asked, "What's your name? I want to thank you properly."

"My friends call me Kent," he replied with a smile.

"Thank you, Kent, for helping us. You will always be welcome at my firepit."

"And you will be welcome at mine," Kent replied.

As Yani, Etta and Cru began to return to their camp, a deep rumble of thunder echoed through the valley.

"Wait," called Kent. "I have a camp in a cave just up the trail. It would be much more comfortable and drier there than camped in the open. Why don't you come stay there?"

"Please, Yani," pleaded Cru. 'I hate sleeping in the rain."

Yani looked from Etta to Cru then said, " Let's go get Deet and the goats. A cave sounds like a much better idea tonight than out in the open. I don't like sleeping wet either."

Yani hurried to Deet as soon as they came into the campsite. Shaking him she said, "Deet, wake up. There is a storm coming and we have had the luck of being invited to share a cave tonight. As soon as we can get things packed up again, we need to get moving. We want to get there before the storm breaks."

Before she had finished another clap of thunder echoed through the river gorge. Cru and Etta had already caught the goats and with Kent's help they quickly had their goods gathered up.

Yani explained as they followed Kent that they would be much more comfortable in the cave. Deet didn't argue with her.

Rud and Ren were arguing about how they should get lose. Yani had done a good job of tying them to the tree. She had Kent wrap their arms around a tree, then tied their hands together. Not only could they not move from this spot but they could not reach the ropes with their mouths. Chewing through the ropes was not an option. The only thing they could do to get loose was reach the knife she had placed there and saw the rope in two.

"Can you feel the knife?" asked Rud. "If you can then pick it up and hand it to me so I can cut my ropes."

"I can just reach it. Let me see if I can get a good hold on it," said Ren as he strained to grasp the knife. "Ouch! Blast it, it cut me."

"Good," replied Rud. "That means it's sharp. Now pick it up and hand it to me."

"I don't think so," replied his companion. "I'm going to cut my ropes then I'll cut you free."

"Don't you trust me?" asked Rud.

"To be perfectly honest, not in the least. I've known you too long. I can just imagine you getting free, then walking away and leaving me here."

"Alright. Have it your way but would you just hurry up. It's starting to rain."

Ren worked franticly to cut himself loose. As he worked the blade got harder to hold. Adjusting his grip on the knife he realized it was wet. "Darn, where I cut my finger it's bleeding. It's making the blade hard to hold."

"Then give it to me. I want to get out of this mess so I can go after that knapper woman and the rest of that bunch. I'm going to kill them all. Starting with Kent. I should have drowned him back when we drowned Lei. Now give me that blade."

Rud struggled with Ren trying to take the knife away from him. Ren held on as hard as he could knowing his life depended on his keeping it. But the blade was too slick from his blood and it slipped from his hand. As he lost his hold on it so did Rud. The knife fell to the ground. When it hit the wet leaves it slid away, just out of reach of the outlaws.

"I told you to hand it to me. Now see what you've done. I can't believe how stupid you are sometimes. Now pick the cussed blade up and hand it to me this time," yelled Rud.

Ren tried to find the blade again. He felt all around on the ground behind them. Finally, his finger just barely touched it. No matter how hard he tried, he could not quite reach it.

"Come on," whined Rud. "Get ahold of it and give it to me."

"Rud, you can yell and threaten all you like but we're stuck here. I can't reach it."

"What do you mean you can't reach it. You got it before," asked Rud, a note of panic creeping into his voice.

"Just what I said. I can't reach it. When you knocked it out of my hands it slid away from us. Just far enough that I can't reach it. Our only hope now is that Kent will take pity on us and come back to cut us loose."

Rud went quiet for a bit. Finally, he said, "Do you think there's a chance he'll do that?"

"What do you think?"

The sky was starting to get light when Ren was jolted awake. He had been dreaming of swimming in the river back home. The water was way too cold and he wanted to get out so he could get warm. He tried and tried to move toward the bank but a branch from a downed tree kept holding him back. When he woke, he was shocked to see that the river had risen during the night and was lapping at his legs.

"Rud, wake up!" he yelled "Now! We have to get loose and get out of here."

"What? Where am I?" mumbled Rud as he struggled to awaken. When he did, he was terrified at what he saw. The river had overflowed its banks and was rapidly rising. "Ren, you have to get that knife. We have to get loose or we're going to drown."

"Rud, I think the gods have finally decided they've given us enough time to mend our ways."

The first raindrops began to fall as the travelers reached the mouth of the cave. As they entered, Kent stirred up the embers in the firepit and added more wood. Yani and Etta settled the goats near the opening so they could wander in and out to graze on the few weeds that grew there. Wolf made a circuit of the cave and finding it safe, settle by the fire. Black was more cautious and settle near the mouth, watchful of all that was going on.

Deet squatted down by the fire. "Alright, will someone tell me what's going on. I know there is more here than meets the eye. Cru is too quiet. Etta seems upset. And who is this stranger?" with that Deet pointed at Kent. "Why did he invite us to share his cave? Yani, explain it to me."

"Well, it's a rather long story so let me get us something to eat first and then I'll explain," Yani said. She began to dig through her pack for the pouch of acorn meal.

"He saved our lives!" blurted Cru from where he sat with Black and watched the rain.

"He what?" demanded Deet.

"Nothing," mumbled Cru as he buried his face in Black's fur.

"Yani, you need to explain now. Etta can see to the food."

"Alright. But as I said it is a long story. I guess I need to start with that time I went to my old beach to get flint. You remember. When the outlaws were there. Then later I went back to teach one of them to make blades so they wouldn't be such a threat to me. Well, Kent is the young outlaw I taught to make blades."

"Now let me get this straight. You are saying this is one of the outlaws who threatened to kidnap you and force you to make blades for them. And now we just breeze in here and make polite with him. Is everyone losing their minds?" asked a very puzzled Deet.

As Etta quietly stirred the acorn meal into the hot water, she whispered, "There's more to it than that, Deet. Please listen to Yani."

Glaring at the girl, he turned to Yani, "This had better be good."

"Cru is right that Kent saved them. Or at least helped me to save them. The other two outlaws had captured Etta and Cru and planned to hold them hostage to force me make blades they could barter or use to hunt or something. Anyway, they had caught the children and Kent was attempting to get the outlaws to release them. Between the two of us we got them loose."

"And just where are the other two outlaws?" asked Deet.

"We left them tied to a tree," said Cru. "But it's alright because they are very bad, mean men. Right Etta?"

"We had just gotten them tied up when we heard the thunder," said Etta from the firepit.

"And so, when Kent offered shelter in his cave, I accepted," finished Yani.

"We had to tie up the bad men so they wouldn't follow us," explained Cru. "They were really bad. I was scared."

"Ssh," said Yani. "It's alright now. Do you understand now, Deet?"

"I understand what happened. But I don't like it." Turning to Kent, Deet said, "Thank you for sharing your shelter but I have to admit I'm uncomfortable with sharing a shelter with an outlaw. Even one who saved Cru and Etta. How did you come to be banished anyway?"

Kent gazed into the fire for a few moments before he began. Then looking up at Deet he started his story. "First I want to say I am guilty of what I was accused. I know now that it was wrong. I'm not trying to make excuses. That said, here's my story. It happened like this. When I was twelve summers Rud and Ren were the big men in my village. At least I thought they were. What they really were though, were bullies. I followed them around and wanted to be tough like them. All summer they had been pushing the younger boys around. One afternoon we were swimming in the river when one of the younger boys they liked to pick on showed up. It was a very hot day so Lei, the boy they picked on, couldn't pass up a chance to cool off just because we were there. He waded into the river and started floating in the cool water. As soon as he was into the deep part of the river, Rud swam up behind him and pushed him under. Ren joined him and they held him under for an awfully long time. I pleaded with them to let him up but they just laughed. Finally, they let him go but he didn't come up. We all three dove down looking for him but we never found him. I was getting ready to run to the village for help when Rud grabbed me. He told me if I ever told anyone what happened they would make me regret it. So being a coward I held my tongue. That night when Lei didn't return home the village elders began making the rounds of the village asking if anyone had seen him. When they came to my house, I said I had no idea what could have happened to him and denied seeing him. What I didn't know was we had been seen. Mya had followed Lei to the river hoping she could swim too until she saw Rud and Ren were there. She was waiting in the woods hoping they would go away. She saw everything. The elders agreed I hadn't taken part in the drowning but I hadn't gone for help or told them what had happened. In their eyes I was equally guilty. That is why I was banished."

They were all quiet for a while when Kent had finished. Finally, Cru broke the silence. "But didn't you tell them you were sorry? That you tried to stop them?"

"Yes, Cru, I did and I was deeply sorry but I still had not gone for help. They were right to banish me. I just wish I could have had the courage at the time to have gone off on my own rather than following along behind Rud and Ren. I have been trying to break away from them ever since. It has been five summers and they're still following me. I imagine it's because I have been able to adapt to living on my own and they haven't."

"What are you going to do?" asked Etta. "Live in this cave for the rest of your life?"

"Yes," he said with a sad smile. "That is what I plan to do. Some of the men from the local villages have become friendly and will barter with me for my blades. Even though they know they're not the best blades. But if you need a blade, it's better than nothing. I've found a source of flint just down the river. So, I have what I need. That is except a village."

"I'm sorry you've had to go through that but you seem to have accepted your lot. Hopefully, the villagers will slowly accept you and you can have a village again. But now it's time to sleep," said Yani.

Etta woke during the night to the sound of rain pouring down. Walking to the mouth of the cave, she looked out into the night through the sheet of rain. What she saw troubled her. The river was rising and was close to covering the trail. As she watched, it occurred to her that the water level may rise high enough to reach the outlaws tied to the tree. What if the outlaws had not managed to get free? What would happen if the water reached them? Thinking about where they had left the outlaws, she decided it was on high enough ground that they would be fine even if they didn't get loose. Going back into the cave she wrapped up and went back to sleep.

# Chapter Eleven

The day dawned with a weak watery light. The rain had eased but there was still a gentle drizzle when Cru sat up and looked around. It took him a moment to remember where he was. As the memory of the previous day returned, he sighed, "I hope those bad men got really wet last night."

"I am sure they did," whispered Etta from where she stood at the mouth of the cave. 'Maybe more wet than was good for them. Come look."

Joining her at the entrance Cru was shocked to see that where the trail had been the day before was now a raging river. "Oh, I hope they were able to get loose. Do you think the water got up to where we left them?"

"Yes, I'm pretty sure it did. And if this cave weren't so high up the hillside we would have been wet too. I just hope the river doesn't rise much more or we may be in trouble."

As they watched the water rush by Yani came to join them. "I'm glad we're here in the cave and not back where we were going to camp. It must be under water."

"Do you think the bad men got loose?" asked Cru.

"No, Cru, I don't think they did. But remember what I said about it being up to the gods? Why are they outlaws?" asked Yani.

"Because they drowned that boy," answered Cru.

"Yes," continued Yani. "And now the gods have finished the circle."

Etta and Cru stayed by the mouth of the cave as Yani returned to the firepit to start cooking breakfast.

As the day dragged on, Cru spent it sitting at the mouth of the cave with the goats. From time to time he would pick up a pebble from the gravel that had collected there and toss it into the water. As he watched the water level slowly creep up toward where he sat, he called over his shoulder, "Kent, what do we do if the water keeps coming up until it reaches the mouth of the cave? And if it keeps coming up until it comes into the cave? And even reaches the roof of the cave? What do we do then?"

Kent walked over to where the boy sat and knelt beside him. "Well, do you see that rock there?" He pointed to an odd-shaped chunk of granite well above the water level. "If the water reaches that rock, then we'll leave the cave and head for a safer place. In all the time I've lived here the water has never come up that high but just in case, I made an escape route. Look out that way," he said pointing to the side of the cave entrance. Cru leaned out and looked to where Kent had pointed. "See there's a trail leading along the cliff. Just past the mouth of the cave is a way to climb up the cliff. I cut hand and foot holds into the face of the cliff so we can climb out."

Leaning out and looking where Kent had indicated Cru was able to see where the trail led. "But what about Wolf and Black? And Frisky and Steady? Will they be able to climb out?"

"I am sure the goats will be fine. Have you ever watched them climb? And I think Wolf and Black can make it up the slope, too. If not, they can run along the trail. It is farther but eventually reaches the top. So, your job today is to watch the water and let us know if it reaches that rock. Can you do that?"

"You bet," replied the boy. "I'll let you know when it starts getting close."

As the day stretched on Cru kept a close watch on the water level. Etta and Deet dozed by the fire. Kent settled in the corner of the cave that was his work area and began chipping the flint to make blades. Yani joined Kent and after watching for a while said, "Let me show you something." Taking his hammer stone, she picked up a nodule and began chipping off flakes. "Watch how I hold the hammer stone. If you angle it like this you can get a truer hit. Then the flake is also truer." She chipped off several more flakes. Handing the hammer stone back to him she said, "Now you try it."

As the sun moved past its highest point Cru called out. "Come and look. I think the water is starting to go back down. See there's a line of wet ground above the water."

Etta walked over to join him and said, " You're right it has gone back down. Maybe by tomorrow it'll be low enough we can get back on our way."

"I wouldn't plan on it," said Kent. "Even if the water is low enough that the trail is uncovered, it'll be very wet and muddy. You'll need to wait a couple of days for it to dry out. And even then, it'll be rough going. There'll be downed trees and debris that has washed up on the path."

"Oh, I didn't think of that," said Etta. "I'm glad we have a dry place to camp and enough firewood."


Later that evening after they had eaten, Yani said, "Deet, I think we need a story if you feel up to it."

"When have I ever not felt up to a story. Now let me think a minute to see if I can come up with a good one. Maybe one you haven't heard over and over."

Deet sat looking into the fire while the others settled in. Finally, he began, "Once many summers ago there was a murder of crows -you know, Cru, that is what a group of crows is called, a murder. Anyway, this murder of crows lived in a beautiful valley. They had everything they needed there. Blackberry brambles to feed them in the summer, acorns and beechnuts to eat in the fall and winter, bugs, and worms to eat in the spring. There were huge oak trees they could build their nests in and the best thing was there were no men living in their valley to disturb their peace and quiet."

"That's funny, Deet. Crows are never quiet. They make noise all the time. Caw! Caw! Caw!" laughed Cru.

"And just who is telling this story?" asked Deet glaring at the boy.

"You are," he replied hiding his grin.

"As I was saying before I was interrupted. They lived in a valley where they were not disturbed by men. Each spring the mother crows laid eggs in the nests the father crows had built in the oak trees. As the weather warmed, the eggs would hatch and the baby crows would keep the parents busy demanding bugs and worms and anything else the parents could find to drop in their hungry mouths. Then as the spring turned to summer the baby crows would begin to learn to fly. Soon they were joining their parents in search of their own food. Everyone was happy in this peaceful valley UNTIL…"

"Until what?" asked Cru.

"Until one spring when an egg hatched out and the baby crow was not black like crows are meant to be but snow white. At first the crows did not know what to think of this. How could a crow be the wrong color? Some of the elder crows were for pecking it to death. It was definitely not a normal crow. It had to be a bad omen. It must mean something awful was going to happen. Some of the elders wanted to push it from the nest and let it starve. But the mother crows all objected and convinced the elders that it may also be a good omen. That they should let it grow up and see.

"So, the strange white crow grew. It ate the bugs and worms and anything else its parents brought to it. Soon it was a large, beautiful crow even if it was the wrong color. But there was another problem."

Deet paused here in the story and gazed into the fire. When Cru could stand it no longer, he cried, "Tell us, Deet. What was the other problem?"

"Oh, you want to know the other problem. Well, this strange white crow didn't say 'Caw'. No, what it said was 'Saw! Saw!' Not at all crow-like.

"Then something awful happened. Something just terribly awful happened. The most awful thing the crows could imagine."

Again Deet, paused his story and stared into the fire. He shifted his position and made to stand up.

"Deet! You can't stop the story there. What happened?" cried Cru.

Leaning forward until he was nose to nose with Cru, he whispered, "A group of men moved into the valley."

"Oh, no," gasped Cru.

"Oh, yes," replied Deet, stretching. Soon he settled back in his place and cleared his throat. After a moment he continued the story. "The next thing the crows knew the men were cutting down trees and building houses. And then they were picking the berries and digging up the grasses that provided the seeds the crows like to eat. The crows didn't know what to do at first but the elders all agreed that if they let the men alone the men would leave them alone. Or at least that is what they thought. But, one day when a mother crow was picking berries to feed her babies, a man who was also picking berries noticed her.

" 'Get, you nasty crow. Those are our berries,' he yelled. Then before the mother crow could think what to do at this strange behavior the man took a sling from his pouch and flung a rock hitting the crow and killing it. That was an unbelievably bad thing to do but to make it worse he did not say an appropriate thank you to the crow for giving up its life. And that is not all. He just left it there. He killed for no reason at all. Not for food. Not for protection. He just killed it for selfish reasons.

"When the white crow saw what had happened, he swooped down at the man calling, 'Saw! Saw! Saw!' When the man saw the strange white crow and heard its call, he dropped his berry basket and ran back toward the village. When the village elders heard what he had done and about the white crow they were terribly upset. They gathered in the village chief's house to discuss what to do. They talked all the rest of the day and into the night. It was definitely a message from the gods. But what did it mean? A white crow and it cried that it had seen what the man had done. Finally, as the sun was coming up they had reached a conclusion. The man who had killed the crow must go to the dead crow and ask forgiveness. Then he needed to bury the crow. When this had been done, all the men needed to gather and promise the crows that they would never again kill one of their family just for eating the food the gods had provided for them all.

"So, the man who had committed the murder in the murder, went to the crow and after apologizing carried the dead crow to a place under a large oak tree and buried the bird. As he did the white crow flew over and again called, 'Saw! Saw! Saw!'

"That night when the crows all returned to their roosts in the oak trees it was agreed by all the crows that the white crow was a good omen. And the valley was once more peaceful again. But not necessarily quiet."

"And now we need to get some sleep," said Yani. "Tomorrow is another day."

# Chapter Twelve

For three more days, the travelers sheltered in the cave. Yani spent much of the time working with Kent making blades. Deet took advantage of this forced halt in their journey to rest and recover completely from his ordeal with the avalanche. Cru had taken his charge to monitor the water level seriously and spent his time at the mouth of the cave throwing pebbles as he watched. Etta was the only one who became restless. After she had paced back and forth for much of the morning, she said, "I can't stand this! I have to get out of this cave. I think I'm going to go check out Kent's escape up the side of the cliff."

"If you do be very careful. The rain may have weakened my hand holds. If so, you could take a nasty fall," advised Kent. "Cru, why don't you go with her?"

"Let's go!" said Cru jumping to his feet.

The young people had only been gone a short time when Yani heard them returning. She had expected them to be gone much longer, exploring the area. Cru burst into the cave first, laughing, "You should see Etta. She's covered with mud."

Sure enough when Etta stomped into the cave, she was mud from head to toe. "Stop laughing, Cru. It isn't funny. I could have been hurt," she scolded.

"But you weren't and you do look funny," he insisted.

"Oh, my," exclaimed Yani. "You are a mess. Let me get that old deer skin from my pack for you to wrap in when we get you clean, then I'll help you and we can go down to the water's edge.. If we're careful, I think we can manage that. Cru, you stay here. One muddy child is enough. "

Yani and Etta carefully picked their way down the trail to the edge of the river. It had returned to its normal flow by now and the layer of mud it had left, had been nearly washed away by the gentle rain that had fallen constantly since the flood. When they reached the river, Etta stripped off her dress and handed it to Yani.

While Yani rinsed the mud from her dress, Etta waded into the river being careful to stay in the shallows. As she washed the mud off, Yani asked her, "Why are you so restless. I would think you would be enjoying this time of rest after all the walking we've done."

"I am in a way but, Yani, I keep thinking about the outlaws. What if they didn't get loose? Does that make us murderers? I'd feel better it I knew one way or the other."

"Whatever happened was in the hands of the gods. You need to forget about it. We left them with a knife so they could cut themselves loose. If they didn't then there was a reason that they didn't. Now come out of the water and wrap up in that skin and let's get you back near the fire where it's warm. Your dress is not going to be dry for a while so you won't be going anywhere again soon anyway."

The next morning as the first light of morning crept into the cave, Cru woke to find Etta gone. At first, he thought she had gone to the spring to get fresh water for breakfast but the cooking pot she used to fetch water was still in its place by the fire. He walked over to the mouth of the cave to see if he could see her but she was nowhere in sight. Not wanting to alarm the others he took his place by the mouth of the cave to watch and wait. The others were still asleep when he saw Etta emerging from the woods along the trail. As soon as she reached him, he whispered, " Where have you been? I was worried about you."

As she dropped to the ground by him, she said, "I had to know if the outlaws got away before the flood reached them."

"And did they?" asked the boy.

"No." said Etta.

They sat in silence for a time and finally Cru asked, "Did we kill them?"

"I don't know, Cru. Yani says it was in the hands of the gods but we were the ones who tied them up. But then they were trying to hurt or maybe kill us. And they did kill that boy to get banished. It's all very confusing. I'm glad they're not going to be following us anymore. But I'm sorry they're dead. I just wish I could be sure what we did was right."

When the others woke, Etta had a morning porridge ready for them. As they sat around the fire and ate, Deet said, "I think things have dried out enough for us to return to our journey."

"I'm ready to move on," said Yani. "And I was thinking, Kent, you don't have to stay here in this cave. I've been looking at your outlaw scars and they're not so visible that people would notice. I think either because you were so young it healed cleanly or the men who marked you took pity and didn't cut deeply enough. It could easily pass for just a scratch from a passing branch."

"You're right that they didn't cut me as deeply as the other two. And they didn't rub ash into my wound like they did with Ren and Rud. I think too that the cream that our medicine woman gave me before I was driven out of the village helped it heal cleanly," said Kent.

"Do you want to join us?" asked Yani.

Kent looked at her in stunned silence. "Do you mean that you would let me become one of your group?"

"That's exactly what I mean. We're planning to go across the Steppe to the Mountains That Are Always White. It's a long walk but we would welcome your company."

"And I'm sure they would welcome you into their tribe if you chose to stay with them. The last time I was there, it's been several summers ago now, their village had been nearly wiped out by a sickness. I'm sure they would welcome a strong young man who could hunt and especially one who could also make blades. What do you think? Would you like to join us?" asked Deet.

"Yes," Kent replied. "You have no idea how lonely it is living here all alone."

"Yes, I do have an idea," said Yani with a smile. "I lived alone on my beach to the north for a very long time. But since I had

Wolf, I was never really alone." And with that she reached over and scratched Wolf behind the ears.

As the light crept into the cave the next morning our travelers were packed and ready to resume their journey south.

# Part 3

# The Mountains That Are Always White

# Chapter One

The first warmth of spring was in the air when the travelers reached the last village before the Steppes. Deet had spent time in this village when he had last crossed to the Mountains That Are Always White so they were welcomed there. It was from this village that he had escorted the two young medicine women to their new house south of the Steppes. Both medicine women from the two villages to the south of the Steppes had died from the disease that had wiped out Gyla's village and killed many in the home village of Yani's mother. The group again stopped to rest here before starting the dangerous trek across the vast grass lands.

While there they stayed with the village head man. It was usual for guests of a village to be housed with the head man and in this case Deet had made friends with him over the years of his travels. As they sat around the fire on the night before they were to start their passage across the Steppes, the talk turned to the journey ahead.

"It's not often that we cross the Steppes this time of year. And never in the summer," said the head man

"Why is that?" asked Kent.

"The simple reason is that by now the grass has started to grow and makes it hard to see the markers. You remember how to follow the stones, don't you, Deet?" he asked.

"I remember well. But I have always crossed in winter when the grass was beaten down by the wind and snow," Deet replied.

"I can see why that would be a problem," added Yani. "When I crossed as a child with the Knapper it was the stones that showed us the way. But the snow nearly killed us. We got trapped in a blizzard before we got across. Luckily, we were near enough that we could see the mountains and head for them or we wouldn't have survived. As it was Knut almost didn't survive."

"I found them in the cave shelter that's just off the path once you are across the Steppes. Knut had the coughing sickness and this one, who was only a slip of a girl, was taking care of him. How she got him off the Steppes and to shelter I'll never know, but she did."

"You will need to be very careful to not miss a stone. Especially at the beginning. Once you get far enough south to see the mountains, they will help guide you so you don't end up going in circles. Also remember that water is life. If you miss a water source you will be in trouble. Drink your fill each time you come to a spring and make sure all your water gourds are full before you leave one of the sources. But you know that."

"Yes, we do but it is always good to get a reminder," said Yani. "And this is the first time these three have crossed so they need to hear it."

The next morning as they were preparing to leave the village, the head man came to see them off. "Here," he said handing Deet two full water gourds. "You can never have too much water this time of year."

"Thank you," said Deet as he added them to the baskets on the goats. "They may save our lives if the springs are low. Goodbye, my friend."

The head man watched until they were out of sight, then he returned to his house. As he entered his wife said, "So they are gone."

"Yes, and I hope they make it. This is a hard time to make the crossing but not as hard as it would be in another moon."

# Chapter Two

As they left the forest, Deet walked along the edge of the grass until he found a large stone that seemed out of place. "Here it is," he said to Yani. "This is where we start."

Before they started out across the grass covered plain Yani attached a rope to each of the goats. Handing the leashes to Etta she said, "We can't let them wander. They could wander too far from us and get lost. We'll have to keep them on a lead until we've crossed. Wolf and Black can wander. They will be able to find us but the goats won't."

The grass was knee high as they headed out into the Steppes. Deet and Yani knew what to expect but the others had never seen this vast expanse of grass. As they stepped out on the prairie Etta said, "It reminds me of the sea but it's waving grass rather than water."

"I think the same," said Yani. "It was frightening when I crossed it with Knut as a child. I was sure we would get lost. And this time we may if we aren't careful."

"Notice I'm being careful to walk in a straight line from where we entered the Steppes. Remember the stone I remarked on when we stepped into the grass. That was the first marker. There's a second one up ahead that we must find. To be on the safe side. I think we should walk in a line. Cru and Etta you move an arm's length apart on that side of me," said Deet pointing to his left. "And Yani and Kent, you do the same on that side. If we walk spread out like that, we will be less likely to miss a marker."

"But if we're walking in a straight line, couldn't we just keep going like that? Why do we need markers?" asked Cru.

"Not all the markers tell you to go straight. Some tell you to turn one way or another. They'll lead us to the springs and to slightly sheltered camp sites. You'll see. Sometimes the stones direct us to where the grass is shortest to make walking easier. The old ones who marked the path were incredibly wise."

It was nearing midmorning when Cru called out, "Stop, Deet. I think you missed a stone. Look, isn't this a marker?"

Walking over to the boy, Deet said, "You're right that is a marker. It's a good thing we're spread out like this or we would have missed it. I thought I was walking in a very straight line but I guess not. That is not good."

"I was pretty sure you were not walking straight," said Kent. "When we started, I picked out a spot ahead of me and when we got to it I was just a little bit from where I thought I should be."

"But I was so sure I was walking straight," said Deet.

"Deet, I think it's your limp. Since the avalanche you've been limping so you take a longer step with your right leg than your left. That would make you walk a little bit sideways. Maybe one of us should be the one in the middle," said Etta.

Deet looked at the marker then stared off toward the southern horizon. After a while, he said, "As much as I hate to admit it, I think you're right. Which of you want to take the middle?"

"I think it should be Kent, "said Yani. "He was able to determine that we were off a bit before Cru even found the marker. We can't risk being off and missing a stone. At least not until we can see the mountains."

"So, Kent, are you willing to take the middle," asked Deet.

"I guess so. But I still want us to walk spread out like we have been doing. That way one of us will be sure to find the marker."

Deet checked the marker to make sure it was telling them to go straight ahead and not a turning marker, then he moved to the end of the line. Now they were walking with Deet on one end, then Yani, Kent and Cru. Etta was on the other end. "I think we should all start picking a point to walk toward as a check on each other. We don't dare stray from the way," said Yani.

Making sure they were keeping the same distance between them they started again on their southward journey. When they reached the next marker, Kent nearly tripped over it. Relieved that their plan was working, they checked the marker and then moved on. When the sun was at its high point in the sky, they reached a marker indicating a shift in direction. Looking off to the west, the direction the marker indicated, said Yani, "I think we should rest a bit. I'm tired and I think the rest of you may be, too."

"Plus, the goats should graze a while. They keep pulling on the leads because they want to eat," said Etta. "I am tired of fighting them. I need a break for a while.

When they had dropped down onto the ground, Yani handed them each a piece of jerked venison to eat. "We each need to drink some water but be careful not to spill any. Until we know the output of the springs, we need to use the water very sparingly. We may need to make the water we have last many days."

When they started out again, after their rest, the line moved off to the west. As they walked the ground dipped slightly.

They stopped for the night as the evening star appeared in the west. They had not missed a marker stone since the first one that luckily Cru had seen before they had gone too far off course. As soon as they had eaten some jerked venison and drank a little water, they curled up in their sleeping cloaks and were soon asleep. A long day of walking plus the stress of nearly missing a marker guaranteed them all a good sound sleep.

As the sun rose, they prepared for another day of travel on the Steppes. They formed the same line as the day before and continued the trek across the sea of grass. Kent was very careful to walk as straight as possible and by midmorning they had passed two more markers. Each of these markers indicated they should continue in the same direction.

The third marker had them turn slightly back to the east. Yani hoped it was directing them to the first spring since she was very concerned to know if they would find water or if they would have to make what they had last for the whole crossing. Late in the afternoon the land dipped into a small valley. There they found not only another marker but the first spring. It was not a robust spring but water did trickle out of the ground and ran over a rock before forming a tiny stream.

"It's not long before we begin to lose the light so I think we should camp here for the night," said Deet. "With such a slow trickle of water it will take a while to refill our drinking gourds. What do you think?"

"I agree," said Yani. "Etta, will you tend to the goats, please. Cru I have a job for you, too. Gather the drinking gourds and I want you to hold each one under the water where it trickles over the rock and fill them. Make sure you fill them all the way to the top. We can drink our fill from one of them this evening and then refill it again before we sleep."

As they each went about their tasks, Black slipped off to hunt. Kent had a small fire burning in the firepit someone had made by the spring. Yani filled a cooking pot and made some acorn porridge. When it was bubbling on the fire, she added a handful of dried berries. It would make a nice break from the jerked venison they had been eating.

As the stars appeared in the sky, Cru whispered to Etta, "I'm worried. Black's not back yet. I hope he's not lost."

Hugging the boy to her, she whispered back, "Black will find his way back. His nose will lead him home. And if we're lucky, he'll bring back a nice fat rabbit for our breakfast. Remember how Yani has told us how Wolf would go off and hunt for them as they crossed the Steppes. And Black has brought back game for Wolf several times. I promise you, Black will find you no matter what."

"Yes, but Black has never been on the Steppes before. And, I would never say this in front of him, but Black's not as smart as Wolf."

"He may not be as smart as Wolf," chuckled Etta, "but he is smart enough to find his way home to you."

Cru was just beginning to doze off when something plopped on his face. Starting up, he yelled, "Ahhh, what's that? What's attacked me? Help!" Jerking up he came eye to eye with Black. Looking around he realized that Black had dropped a freshly killed rabbit on his face.

"See I told you he'd be back. And he brought you a present. Let's see if we can talk Kent into cleaning it while I build up the fire. We can spit it and let it slow cook over night. I can almost taste it now. Warm juicy rabbit for breakfast."

The travelers woke the next morning to not only the sun shining in their eyes but the smell of fresh cooked rabbit. The rabbit did not offer a lot of meat but they each got a fair share including both Wolf and Black. As they ate, each of the humans praised Black. Cru was hoping all the praise would encourage him to bring them more game.

Two days later they reached the next water source. They had not moved as rapidly as they had hoped but still were making decent time. It was only midafternoon but they decided to make camp anyway. There was a small stream that trickled out of the ground before running a short distance then disappearing into the tall grass. Cru quickly filled all the water gourds while the others were busy with their tasks around camp. When he had finished with the water, Cru began to explore the area.

Seeing him wandering off, Yani called. "Don't go far Cru. It's easy to get lost here. Make sure you keep us in sight. Do you hear me?"

" I hear you and I'll be careful. I'm not going far. And I'll keep making sure I can see you." With that he waved and began walking away slowly.

Etta kept an eye on him for a while and decided he wasn't going to wander too far. Since she had her tasks completed, she laid back in the grass to doze in the sun. It wasn't long before all the travelers were stretched out in the grass snoozing. It was too early to start the fire since wood was scarce so there was no smoke to mark their location. The goats also had laid down to rest and eat the grass they could reach without moving. Black had gone off to hunt and Wolf was in his usual spot beside Yani. With all of them stretched out in the grass napping, they had disappeared from view.

In the meantime, Cru's interest had been captured by an insect. It was one he had never seen before- a beetle of some sort and when the sun hit its back it shone a beautiful iridescent green. If he moved slightly the color would change to purple. As he watched it crawl along, he moved in circles around it. He had lost track of the time but was sure he hadn't been away from camp for long. Since he hadn't walked far, he wasn't in a hurry to return to camp. Finally, when he lost interest in the beetle, he stood up and looked around. To his horror the camp was nowhere to be seen. All he saw was a wide sea of waving grass. The camp had vanished.

He stood puzzled, trying to decide which way to go. He took a couple steps in one direction then stopped. He wasn't sure if this was the right way. He had circled the beetle so many times he no longer knew which he should go to reach the camp. He stood very still and listened. All he could hear was the swishing sound of the wind through the grass. He called out to Etta but he didn't get an answer. The wind had blown his cry away. Panic started to set in as he realized he was lost. Every direction he looked was exactly the same. Then an awful thought hit him. What if they had left him? Would that be possible? Could they have left him alone on this vast sea of grass? If they had left him, he would never find his way off the Steppes. Could letting him wander off have just been a ruse so they could slip off without him. As fear took over, he dropped down into the grass and curled up into a ball. As the tears slowly ran down his cheeks, he was overcome with terror.

In the meantime, Etta awakened from her nap and looked around for Cru. Not finding him in camp she scanned the horizon looking for the boy. When she couldn't find him, she awakened Kent. When he opened his eyes, she whispered, "Kent, we have a problem. Cru isn't back and I can't see him. He may have wandered off too far. I don't want to wake Yani or Deet yet. Will you help me find him?"

"Of course but maybe we need more help that just us," he said as he pointed to Wolf.

"You're right. Wolf, come," Etta called softly. Wolf stood and walked stiffly to Etta. She knelt by him and said, "Find Cru. He's lost and we need to find him."

Wolf whined softly then began walking slowly off into the grass. As he walked, he sniffed the ground. Etta walked by his side out though the grass and soon she heard a muffled crying. As she reached the top of a gentle rise, she found Cru curled on the ground sobbing.

Kneeling by him she scooped him up in her arms. "Hey," she said, "It's all right. Wolf and I found you."

"I looked for you and you'd all disappeared. I thought you'd left me," he sobbed.

"Cru, look at me. I promise I will never go off and leave you. I didn't realize that when we all laid down you wouldn't be able to see us. We didn't go anyplace. We were all waiting for you at the camp."

Setting him on his feet, she said, "Come on, let's get back to camp before the others wake up."

Cru was quieter than usual during the evening and to Yani's surprise he wrapped in his sleeping cloak for the night before anyone else. She approached him and gently felt his forehead. Finding it cool she asked, "Are you feeling sick, Cru?"

"I'm only tired, Yani. I'm really all right," he replied before pulling the cloak tighter around himself.

Yani looked at Etta for an answer but she just smiled and shrugged. "Maybe he just got worn out wandering around today. I'm sure he will be fine tomorrow."

During the night Etta felt a hand on her shoulder. Opening her eyes, she saw Cru looking down at her. "Are you awake, Etta."

"I am now," she said. "What's wrong?"

"Every time I fall asleep, I keep having the same bad dream," he whispered. "Can I sleep with you?"

Etta lifted the edge of her sleeping cloak and the boy slid in. Wrapping her arms around him, she pulled him close. His body was trembling. "So, tell me what was so scary about your dream."

"I dreamed that I was all alone in the middle of the Steppes. Then I see you or Yani or Deet off in the distance. I start running toward you and I run and run but I can't catch up with you and finally you disappear. I wake up crying. As soon as I go back to sleep, I have the same dream all over again."

"Well, I have a good tight hold on you now and I'm not going any place." Rubbing his back, she hummed to him until he finally fell asleep.

When the sun woke her the next morning, she was surprised to find Yani looking down at her. "What's Cru doing sleeping with you?" she asked.

"It's a long story," Etta answered. "I'll tell you as we fix breakfast."

As soon as Yani had returned to preparing the morning porridge, Etta joined her and in a whisper told her of Cru's scare the day before. When they had the porridge ready, Etta gently shook Cru to wake him. As soon as he woke, he started up and looked around. "You're all right," reassured Etta. "It's just time to get up and get on the way. Yani has porridge ready. And you need to make sure the water gourds are full."

Cru scrambled to his feet and picking up his water gourd walked over to the stream to begin his task.

They were slow getting on the trail that morning. For some reason they all seemed reluctant to leave the camp. The air was heavy and clouds had begun to build in the east. As they walked in their line, a gentle wind began blowing from the east. When they reached the first marker it was not Kent who found it but surprisingly it was Etta.

"Stop" she cried. "We have a problem. Look. Here is the mark. Kent you're not walking in a straight line now."

The others gathered around her, and sure enough, the marker was at her feet. "But I was being so careful," said Kent. "I've been so successful at staying in a straight line. Why did I fail this time?"

"It's the wind," said Cru. "It started blowing right after we started walking. And it keeps getting stronger."

"I did notice the wind but didn't think it would make that much of a difference," said Kent. "So, what do we do?'

As they pondered the problem, there was a rumble of thunder in the distance. "It looks like we're going to have to hunker down when that reaches us. Until it does, let's move on carefully but I'll walk on the other side of Etta," said Yani. "That way we have a better chance of hitting the marker. What do you think, Deet?"

"I think that will work unless the wind picks up more," he replied.

They started out once more with Yani on the end. As they moved out each one was very aware of the wind. It remained steady for most of the morning and when they reached the next marker it was Cru who found it.

"It looks like we're doing a better job of walking straight," said Deet. "Let's keep walking until the wind gets stronger or the rain starts, then we can hunker down."

They had just reached the next marker when a flash of lightening followed by a loud clap of thunder made them jump. "I think we need to hunker down now!" said Yani. "We're the tallest things for as far as I can see and the tallest thing is what the lightening will hit." Pulling their sleeping cloaks out of their packs, they squatted down on the ground. Once they were settled each of them pulled their sleeping cloaks over their heads. By the time the rain started they were prepared for the downpour.

The storm seemed to go on forever. Even the animals sought what shelter they could by moving as close to the humans as possible. Cru found he had the most shelter since not only Black but both goats had crowded against him. He lifted the edge of his cloak and put it over Black keeping him at least a little drier. Finally, as the sun was setting, the worst of the storm had passed. The lightning and thunder had moved on and the rain had died to a gentle shower. They prepared to spend a damp uncomfortable night.

When dawn broke it brought a bright clear sky. Etta was the first to crawl out from under her cloak. She stretched and looked around. As she slowly surveyed the Steppes, she stopped in amazement. Before her was the sight she had been longing to see since she was a little girl. On the southern horizon was a line of mountain peaks covered with a new layer of snow. Shaking Cru awake she cried, "Cru, wake up. Look! We are almost there. I can see the mountains."

Pulling his sleeping cloak from over his head he stood and looked where Etta was pointing. "I see them. They're so close. I bet we'll be there by tonight. And we can just walk without worrying about the markers. We can see the mountains and just walk toward them."

"I'm afraid you are a bit optimistic there, Cru," said Deet emerging from his sleeping cloak. "It will be at least three days before we get off the Steppes. If the weather stays this clear we can just walk but what if the mountains disappear into the clouds again. We will still follow the markers at least until we can see the end of the Steppes."

"But they're so close," said Cru.

"I'll tell you what. Tell me at the end of the day if you still think we'll be there tonight," replied Deet with a laugh.

As soon as they could get packed up and moving, the travelers headed south again. They continued using the same walking pattern they had used since they entered the Steppes. The only change was since the wind had died down, Yani returned to her original walking order. They had no trouble finding the markers and were making good progress. They stopped midday to rest and eat some jerky. As they rested, Yani asked, "So, Cru, do you still think we'll be off the Steppes tonight?"

"What I think is someone is moving those mountains. They aren't getting any closer. I just don't understand," said Cru.

Laughing, Yani replied, "I felt the same way when I came this way with the Knapper. And imagine by this time we had been through a blizzard and Knut was extremely sick. From about here until I got him off the Steppes, I was almost carrying him. After a couple of days, I had to abandon his pack. I couldn't help him and carry both of our packs. Thankfully Deet showed up with it after we had gotten to the cave."

"I am still amazed that you managed to get him to the cave. Remember she was not much older than you are, Cru. But she did it all by herself."

"Why didn't you put him on Wolf's traveling pack?" asked Cru.

"That is easy. I hadn't taught Wolf to pull a traveling pack yet. I did that when we got to the mountains. And now we need to get moving again or we'll never get off this sea of grass."

# Chapter Three

Toward the end of the third day after seeing the mountains for the first time, Deet pointed out a dark line separating the grass from the base of the mountains. "See that. Cru? That's the forest we'll walk through after we leave the Steppes. Now I can safely say we'll be off the Steppes early tomorrow."

"At last!" cried Cru. "I'm really tired of grass."

"In two more days we'll be in a house and maybe the men can even go hunting and get us some fresh meat. That would be very welcome," said Yani.

They walked until the stars began to show in the sky, then they made a cold camp and bedded down for the night. As soon as the sun rose the next day, they were on the move again and as Deet had predicted they came to the end of the Steppes before midday. It seemed strange to be on a clearly, visible trail. The darkness of the woods was almost frightening after the many days of wide-open spaces. When they reached the small path that led up to the cave, the travelers turned off the main trail and climbed up to the shelter.

They were happy to find a small pile of wood near the firepit. As Kent and Deet tended to the goats, Cru gathered some more wood and Etta went to the stream to fetch some water for porridge. Soon they were settled around a fire with a warm bowl of porridge. As they were eating Black slipped out of the cave into the night.

"Now if Black is as good as Wolf was, he'll bring a nice young deer back for us," said Deet.

"That's right. You did bring me a deer that night didn't you, Wolf. Did you give Black instructions to do the same?" asked Yani with a smile. Then she leaned over and gave Wolf a hug. As she scratched him behind the ears he whined softly. "I know, we're both getting old, aren't we, boy."

They had settled down for the night when Black slinked back into the cave. He hadn't brought a deer but he did bring the remains of a large hare. He had eaten his fill then brought the rest back to Wolf. Giving Yani an embarrassed look, Wolf carried the gift over near the mouth of the cave and enjoyed the first fresh meat he had had in days.

The next morning, they continued on their way. They were hoping to make it to Gyla's village by midafternoon. Yani knew that Gyla was no longer there but she would always think of it as Gyla's village. It was sad to think that a sickness had killed everyone in the village except Hava. Deet had said that people had started coming back to the village when he had last been here so they were expecting a warm welcome.

Late afternoon they finally walked into a silent village. Looking around they found it abandoned. Kent entered a couple of houses and each time came out to report that they were empty and the firepits were cold. Finally, they entered the house that Yani and the Knapper had shared the summer they had spent here and prepared for the night. Kent and Cru went in search for some firewood while Deet cleaned out the firepit so they could get a fire going as soon as they got back.

Once they had a nice fire burning, Yani said, "I guess we need to move on to my uncle's village soon. I hope they are still there. I can't imagine where everyone has gone. It's obvious nobody lives here anymore."

"I'm puzzled, too. The village was coming back to life when I was last here," said Deet.

"Well, we can't do anything about it tonight. Let's settle in and deal with it tomorrow," said Yani.

"I'm thinking it might be a good idea to rest here for a couple days before moving on. If we do, Deet and I can go hunting," said Kent. "It would do us all good to have some fresh meat."

"That's a good idea," said Cru. "I can go with you and help you."

"Maybe you can stay here and be of more help," said Deet. "I've been in the forest with you before and if you come you'll scare off any game within a day's walk."

"But I can be quiet," protested Cru. "Please."

"I have a better idea," said Etta. "If I remember right Yani said there were flint nodules in the stream. We could go look for some and if we are lucky, we may even be able to catch a trout. I saw a nice big fat one when I went for water earlier. Do you know how to tickle a trout?"

"I don't want to make them laugh. I just want to catch them so I can eat them," replied Cru.

"Tickling them is the best way to catch them. Tomorrow I'll show you how. That way if the mighty hunters aren't successful on their hunt, we can have fresh trout. I bet we are more successful than Deet and Kent. What do you say? Are you game?"

Deet was standing behind him so Cru could not see the big smile he gave Etta. Deet said "I don't know. I bet we not only have fish tomorrow but we will have a haunch of venison to go with it."

# Chapter Four

Early the next day, Kent and Deet took their spears and leaving the others sleeping moved off into the forest. They walked silently as they followed the trail that climbed toward the base of the mountains. "One summer when I was here, I killed a bear near where the forest gave way to the rocky slopes. I'm not looking to kill one of those today but if we ran across one, I wouldn't mind giving it a try. Have you ever hunted bear?" Deet asked.

"No, the biggest thing I've killed was an elk. Bears are too aggressive for me. And I like the taste of elk and deer much better," replied Kent.

"You're probably right. I'm getting too old to take on a bear, anyway. So, deer or elk it is." Slowing his pace, Deet began looking for a game trail that crossed the path they were on. It wasn't long before they found what they wanted. Crossing at an angle was a well-used trail marked with many deer tracks.

Studying it for a moment, Deet said, "It looks like it will be deer tonight."

"That is, if we can find one. I'd hate to get back empty handed only to find Etta and Cru had caught a nice string of trout," said Kent

"I'd rather get back to a dinner of trout than to have all of us come up empty handed," replied Deet. "Personally, I like to eat no matter who kills it."

"I've noticed," laughed Kent. "And I like to eat, too."

The men moved off the main path to follow the game trail into the forest. They had gone a short way when the trail crossed a small brook. Seeing the number of deer sign, Deet said, "I think if we hide behind those shrubs, we might get lucky and have a deer come to us. This seems to be a popular watering hole."

Wetting his finger, Deet held it up, turning it from side to side. "The wind seems to be coming mostly from that direction," he said, pointing toward the mountains. "If we stay on this side of the stream any deer that comes to drink won't pick up our scent. You go over there and I'll take this side of the thicket."

The hunters took their places and prepared to wait.


Back in the village, Yani had finished cooking some porridge for breakfast. Smelling it, Etta climbed out of bed and moved to the firepit. "That smells good," she said, joining Yani by the fire.

"You did a fine job of distracting Cru from wanting to go with the men to hunt. I'm sure they'll be much more successful on their own. And I would like to have some flint nodules from the stream to work on. We are going to need some more blades to trade on our return to the Valley next year."

"I'm sure I can get you the flint, but I'm hoping we can get a few trout, too."

"I'm sure we can," said Cru as he tumbled out of bed. "I'm ready whenever you are."

"How about we eat some porridge first? I don't know about you but I'm hungry," said Etta tousling his hair. "There's plenty of time. The men will be gone all day. They have to go farther than we do and then find a deer, kill it, bleed it, and then carry it home. We just have to walk a little way out of the village and tickle a fish and snatch it out of the water. We'll win this bet, no problem."

As soon as they had eaten, Etta took two carrying pouches and led Cru to the stream. As they started to follow it, they both looked for likely flint nodules. It wasn't long before Cru found a usable one and started to put it in his pouch. "Wait," said Etta. "Don't put it in the pouch now. Lay it here on this big rock. That way we can see it on our way back. You don't really want to carry a bunch of rocks all the way up the stream and then carry them back down, do you, silly boy."

"No, I don't because that would be just silly, Silly."

"Are you saying I'm silly, Sillier," laughed Etta.

Cru walked along beside Etta laughing. After a while he asked, "Etta, why are you so nice to me?"

"Why, Cru, why wouldn't I be nice to you?"

"Back in the Valley it seemed someone was always yelling at me or scolding me. But since we've been on this journey that almost never happens."

Etta thought for a few minutes then said, "I think it might be because you've grown up a lot on this journey. More importantly you've learned to think before you act. At least most of the time you have. And besides, who else do I have to play with but you?"

"Oh. Etta, are you being silly again?" said Cru.

Just then Etta spotted a trout in the stream. Grabbing his arm, she stopped Cru and pointed. "Look there is a nice big trout. Now be very still and watch what I do." With that she slipped off her moccasins and tucked her dress up into her belt. Entering the water downstream from the fish she very slowly moved up behind it. As she neared it, she let her hands dangle in the water until they were nearly touching the bottom of the stream. As she came up behind the fish, she slowly lifted her hands until her fingers were just barely touching the fish's belly. With a swift movement, she grabbed the fish and tossed it onto the bank. Scrambling out of the water she picked up a rock and hitting the fish in the head killed it. Dropping the rock to the ground she knelt and said the words of thanks to the spirit of the fish. Putting it in her pouch, they continued up the stream.

It wasn't long before they spotted another trout. "Now it's your turn to try. Remember you need to move very slowly and quietly. Take your moccasins off and roll up your pants. Go into the water right here," Etta said pointing to a spot well downstream from the fish.

Cru stepped into the water and froze. Looking at Etta he whispered, "You didn't say the water was freezing cold."

"Do you see that snow on the top of the mountains? That's where this water comes from. Now stop being a baby and catch that fish," Etta said with a big grin.

Shivering, Cru started moving slowly up behind the fish. He was able to get his hands under it but just as he grabbed, it swished its tail and swam beyond his reach. "I almost had it," cried the boy. "Why did it move? What did I do wrong?"

"You didn't do anything wrong. And you are right you almost had it. It hasn't moved far so try again. That was really good for your first try."

It took three more times but finally Cru managed to toss a fish out onto the bank. Etta made sure it did not flop back into the stream as Cru climbed out. "Okay, now take the fish's life and thank its spirit. You must always do that. Do you know the right words?" asked Etta.

"I think so," Cru replied. Kneeling by the fish he whispered, "Thank you, Brother Fish, for giving your life so my family and I can eat. Go in peace." And with that he hit the fish with a large rock and killed it.

"You did well," said Etta. "Now the next one is mine."

By midmorning they had three large trout in their pouch and were ready to start back down the stream collecting flint nodules as they went. When they reached a large flat rock by the stream Etta said, "Let's stop here so I can clean the fish. We don't want to wait and do it back in the village. Fish guts stink."

"Phew, you are right about that," giggled Cru.

"You know it was right around here that Yani taught herself to make blades," said Etta.

"Yani taught herself?" asked Cru. "I thought the old Knapper taught her."

"Well yes and no. The way Deet told the story Yani was worried about the Knapper. He had gotten old and really weak so she decided if she could at least make the flakes for him all he would have to do was to shape them. She was already collecting the flint nodules. So, one day she slipped off when he was sleeping and came far enough up the stream that she didn't think anyone would see her. You know it was tabu for girls to even touch hunting tools."

"But Yani hunts and so do you and nobody says anything," replied Cru.

"Yes, but not where anyone except our village can see. Didn't you ever wonder why Deet is always the one to barter the blades? And why he never tells anyone it's Yani that makes them?" Etta asked.

"I just thought it was because he's a better trader," replied Cru.

"That may be true but if most men knew the blades they were trading for were made by a woman they wouldn't want them. Even though they are better made than what most men can make. She's better than the old Knapper, or so Deet says. Anyway, she came way up this stream. Once she found a few good nodules she started to try her hand at knapping. I guess it took her a few tries but when she thought she had a couple of good flakes to show the Knapper she gathered her things and returned to the village.

"There was only one slight problem. Someone had seen her," said Etta.

"Oh, no," cried Cru. "Did she get in trouble?"

"Patience," said Etta. "I'm getting there. So, when she got back to the village, the Knapper was very worried about her because she had been gone for so long. As she fixed his supper, she began asking him questions about how he learned his trade and how long it took him to learn and so on."

"But did she get in trouble? I have to know," pleaded Cru.

"Who is telling this story?" demanded Etta.

"You are," mumbled Cru.

"That's right. Now just be patient.

"Anyway, as Yani is questioning the Knapper, he notices the little chips of flint sticking to Yani's dress. So he asks her to show him what she had done. When he saw her flakes, he asked how long she had been practicing. She admitted that she had just started that afternoon. He was amazed at how good her flakes were. That's when he said he would teach her but only in their house until they got back to their home by the sea. He didn't want anyone to know what she had been doing.

"But as I said someone had seen her. As Yani was fixing their evening meal, Deet called out and asked to come in. After they had eaten Deet offered to tell a story. The story he told was about a butterfly who taught herself to make honey. The moral of the story was that if the bees found out they would come and sting the butterfly to death. And the butterfly was warned to only make her honey, which was better than what the bees made, far away by the sea. And that is just what Yani did.

"Now let's get these fish back home. I want to have them on the spit cooking when Deet and Kent get back."

As they slowly walked back toward the village, Cru suddenly said, "So that is why Deet calls Yani his little butterfly. That's it, isn't it?"

"I never thought of that but I think you're right. You know, Cru, for a silly boy you can be pretty smart sometimes," said Etta running a few steps ahead of the boy.

When he caught up with her, he gave her a big hug. "I really like you, Etta."

"I guess I have to like you, too, then," said Etta hugging him back.

It was dark when the men got back from their hunt. They had been successful also but it had been late in the day when a deer finally appeared by the water hole. They decided to just bleed it and gut it there and wait until they returned to the village to finish the butchering. They cut a sapling to hang it from and with the deer dangling from the pole between them they returned to the village. They could smell the cooking fish as they entered the village.

"It's a good thing we got this deer or I'm not sure Cru would ever let us live it down. Not that he caught the fish. I'm fairly sure that was Etta's doing," said Deet as they put the deer down.

"Are we going to finish up the butchering tonight or would it be safe to wait until tomorrow?" asked Kent.

"I say we go in and eat some fish then come back out and finish the job. I'm thinking we should get a fire going so we can smoke some. There's too much to eat before it spoils. It's too warm for it to last long."

They lifted the heavy leather curtain that was the door throwing it up over the roof so they could keep an eye on the deer. They didn't want something to come and carry it away as they ate.

As soon as they had finished eating, the men made a large firepit a short distance from the house. While Kent and Etta got the fire going, Deet made a rack out of green saplings. Once the fire was burning, they began the task of butchering the deer. It was a slow process. After they had it skinned they had to cut the meat into strips that they laid across the rack Deet had made. Yani had wrapped a haunch in a damp cloth to keep it cool for them to cook the next day but the rest had to be dried. When the rest of the meat had been laid across the rack to dry in the smokey heat from the fire, it was late into the night. Long before they were finished Cru had grown bored and wandered off to bed.

"One of us should keep watch," said Deet with a big yawn. "Who wants to take the first watch?"

"I will," said Etta. "I slept late this morning and I can always catch up on sleep tomorrow. Go on and get some rest."

She got no argument from any of them. Soon she could hear gentle snoring blending with the night sounds.

# Chapter Five

Deet was turning the strips of venison on the rack so it would dry evenly when he looked up and saw a group of well-armed men walking toward him. Stepping away from the fire, he raised his hands in the universal gesture of peace.

"Welcome," he said. "We found the village empty and have taken advantage of the shelter for a few days' rest. We just came across the Steppes. We hope we have not offered offense in any way."

One of the men who appeared to be the leader stepped forward. "What would bring a stranger to our territory?"

"We are not exactly strangers," replied Deet. "My life mate wished to visit her family in the next village one last time. Yani has an..."

"Did you say Yani? Yani who walks with the wolf? The Knapper's girl?" asked the man.

"Yes, I'm that Yani," she said as she stepped out of the house. "My mother was from the next village. Tank is my uncle."

"Welcome, Cousin. I am the grandson of Tank. My name is Tam. I'm sorry to tell you that he has journeyed to the Otherside. But you and your friends are welcome in our village."

"Please come and sit by the fire. Are you hungry? We have a haunch of venison, trout and as you can see smoked meat. We also have some dried fish from the North Sea. While we eat I wish to hear what has happened in this village. I spent a wonderful summer here when I was a girl. Gyla taught me herb craft that summer."

While the visitors ate, they told the travelers what had befallen this village. Deet had been right that it had started to recover but then strange things started happening. One night a house caught on fire. Everyone got out safely but the family lost everything. Then a pack of wolves came at night and killed most of the sheep that the village had. A child fell into the fire and was severely burned. It was one thing then another. Finally, the shaman decided there was a curse on the village. He said they should leave everything and move to Tank's village. It took a while to build houses for everyone so the people of Tank's village took the refugees in. As soon as they left this place the luck seemed to change. No one has lived here since.

"And so, when one of the young men who had been hunting reported seeing smoke from this village the shaman sent us to investigate. Some of the elders were sure it was ghosts," said one of the men.

"Ghost we are not," said Yani. "At least we're not yet, are we Deet?"

"You're Deet?" asked the leader of the group. "The trader who brought the medicine women after ours died in the sickness?"

"Yes, did they turn out to be good medicine women?"

"They are excellent medicine women. Almost as good as Gyla was," he replied.


When the men were satisfied that the village had not been taken over by spirits of the dead, all but Tam, Tank's grandson, headed back to their village. Joining Yani by the fire, he said, "You are very welcome but it's a long journey to take for a visit. How long do you mean to stay?"

"I've not decided. I know this will be my last journey but I had a desire to see your beautiful mountains once more before I pass over to the Otherside. I may not have come had I known how hard it was going to be. We should have been here at least a moon ago but we ran into many problems. Nonetheless we're here now. So, tell me what has happened in your village."

It was late in the afternoon when the meat had finally dried enough to pack in a storage basket. Tam rose from where he had been entertaining Yani with the history of the village. Stretching he said, "Do you want to start for my village this late or should we wait until tomorrow? We could do it still today but we would have to move quickly and it would be dark when we got there."

"Tam, if you don't think us rude, I would like to stay here. This is the house the Knapper and I lived in when I spent the summer here as a girl. It feels like home to me," said Yani.

"But don't you want to see our village?" asked Tam.

"Yes, I do want to come to your village but for a visit, not to live while I'm here."

"What about all the terrible things that have happened here? Aren't you uneasy about that?"

"I think they were just some ordinary bad things that happen all the time. It's just a lot of them happened in a short time and they came right after you had been through a terrible plague. If it looks like terrible things are going to start happening, we'll change our plan and move. But for now, I would like very much to stay here," said Yani.

"Then if you are willing, I'll spend the night before I head home. That way we can talk some more."

As they were finishing the evening meal, Tam asked, "Deet, you don't by any chance have some blades that the Knapper made before he passed over, do you? We haven't been able to get good blades since you were last here. Some of our young men have tried their hand at knapping but so far none have really mastered the skill."

"I still have one or two that I haven't used for trade but you may want to look at what Kent makes. He has almost mastered the Knapper's technique," said Deet. "Kent, why don't you get a few of the blades you have been making to show to Tam."

"You mean the ones that…" he started to say.

"Yes, the ones you have worked on since you have been here." Turning back to Tam, Deet continued, "Kent has been working with your native flint since he has been here. I'm sure you'll be pleased with what he has done."

"Come on, Kent, I'll help you get the ones that you should show Tam," said Etta as she took his arm and pulled him toward the door.

As they walked out Deet said, "Kent's still a little shy about showing his work but he is really becoming very skilled."

Once Etta and Kent were out of earshot, she whispered, "You must never tell anyone that Yani is the one who has been making the blades. Most men think that it is tabu for a woman to touch a hunting tool let alone make the blade on it. Deet still implies that the Knapper has made the blades he trades."

"But don't they realize the Knapper passed over years ago?" asked Kent.

"Some do but they see the wonderful blades Yani makes and they pretend they don't know she is the knapper now. So, you must pretend that either the Knapper taught you or you learned by studying the blades he made," Etta explained.

"I understand," Kent replied. "And in a way it was the Knapper who taught me. At least he taught me through Yani."

Etta smile at him and said, "Let's get your blades. If you let Deet teach you, not only will you be a good knapper but you may turn out to be a good trader too."

When Etta and Kent returned. Tam was again trying to talk Yani into moving to his village. As they walked through the door, Yani said, "I will visit I promise but for now I want to stay here. And here's Kent with his blades. Come show Tam what you've made."

The next morning Tam bid the visitors goodbye and started back to his village. After he had left, Yani asked Etta if she would like to go with her to gather herbs. There were several that grew here but not farther north in their Valley. Once they had collected the baskets and knives they would need, they left the village and walked off into the forest.

Cru had gone to see that the goats were still tethered where they had left them at the edge of the meadow. He untied them and led them to the stream to drink. He watched them as the slurped up the cold clear water. When they had drunk their fill, he herded them back to the meadow and tied them again. When he was satisfied they were going to be alright, he began to wander back toward the stream. He had only gotten to the edge of the village when Kent called out, "Cru, where are you off to?"

"I thought maybe I would go see if I could tickle a fish like Etta does. Why?" he answered.

"I thought maybe you would like to try to make blades with me," Kent replied. "Are you interested?"

"Am I!" cried Cru. "You would really try to teach me?"

"That's what I said."

"Who wants a stinky old fish anyway!" cried Cru as he ran over to join Kent. When they were settled in the shade of the house Kent had moved in to, Kent said, "You know, Cru, someone is going to have to be the knapper for your Valley after Yani is gone. So I started thinking that you might be just the right man for it. And if you start learning now from me, then maybe she will also help teach you. It takes a lot of patience to get it right but I think you can do it."

"I've never been very patient," said Cru.

"I don't know," replied Kent. "As I see it, you have more patience than you know. I've watched you with the goats and if any critter takes patience, it's a goat. So, let's get started. You already know how to pick out a good flint nodule. That's the first step. The second step is to chip off a good flake."

By the middle of the day, with a lot of help from Kent, Cru had managed to make two usable flakes. When Yani and Etta appeared at the edge of the village, Cru grabbed his flakes and ran toward them calling, "Yani, look what I did. Kent is teaching me to knap. And I have made two flakes that are usable. Or at least almost."

Running up to them he handed Yani the flakes. As she looked them over, Cru rocked back and forth from one foot to the other. When she didn't say anything, Cru asked, "They are alright aren't they? Kent said they were."

"No Cru," said Yani in a disappointed voice. "I am afraid they are not alright."

Cru hung his head and replied, "I was afraid of that. Kent was just trying to make me feel good."

"Well, Cru, when I said they were not alright it's because they are much better than alright. In fact, they are exceptionally good for your first try. And you are right, they are both usable. Now the next step is to finish them. Come on, let's go join Kent and we will talk about what to do next."

Cru looked up at Yani and when he saw her smile, he knew she had just been teasing him. Giving her a big hug, he turned and ran back to Kent calling as he ran, "She said they were good, Kent! Yani said they were good!"

Laughing Kent replied, "I already told you that. Didn't you believe me?"

"I believed you but Yani said they were good, too."

Etta watched Cru and Yani join Kent and she waved to Yani. "I'll get these herbs set to dry. You join the knapping school."

By the end of the day, Cru had managed to finish a flake into a knife. It was not good enough to be used as a trade good but it would make a usable knife for Cru. When he showed it to Deet that evening he was bubbling with pride.

"Cru, I think you have the making of an excellent knapper. In a summer or two I will be trading your blades."

# Chapter Six

"But why do I need to learn the names and uses of all these plants?" asked Etta. "Wouldn't it be more useful if I were catching fish? Or hunting for flint nodules? Or almost anything but studying these plants? It's not like I am going to be a medicine woman, after all."

"You never can tell. You may well decide to become one after I have passed to the Otherside. When I am gone, the Valley will need to have someone to take over," replied Yani.

"Well, then when we get back to the Valley you can train someone," said Etta.

"That is if I get back to the Valley," replied Yani.

"What do you mean, if you get back?"

"Etta, in case you haven't noticed I am getting old. I'm not sure I'll be able to make the journey back to the Valley."

"Then we'll make a traveling pack and Wolf can carry you like he did with the Knapper."

Wolf looked up from the place where he was sleeping in the sun and whined. Laughing Yani said, "I know, Wolf, you're old too and could never carry me back home. But it's alright. You're not going to have to."

"Well, if Wolf can't, maybe we can train Black. He is young and strong."

"No, Etta, when the time comes, if I can't walk on my own, I will not be going. But that's not a problem to be solved now. So, tell me what is this plant and what is it used for?"

Sighing, Etta answered, "That's tansy. It's used to ease aching joints. Also, to settle upset stomachs. And if you rub it on your skin, it keeps insects from biting."

"Very good. Now this one?"

"That is willow bark. It's good for bringing down fever and stopping headache," Etta said.

"And this one?" asked Yani.

The moon had waxed full when Yani decided she was ready to visit her mother's village. The evening she announced her plan to make the trek, she asked, "Who would like to join me? None of you have to go unless you really want to. I am sure I can find my way."

"I want to go," said Etta.

"I'd like to go but I think I need to stay and help Kent make blades," said Cru. "I know he'll need me."

"That's true. I would be hard put to make blades without your help but I plan to go with Yani. I'd like to see if I can do some trading with the blades I've made. So, I guess you'll have to go too so you can help me make the deals," said Kent.

"Well, I guess if you need me to help, I'll go," replied Cru.

Smiling at the boy, Yani said, "That's very thoughtful of you, Cru. Deet, what about you. Do you want to go?"

"I was thinking I may go hunting. We're going to need a deer skin or two to make new moccasins before we begin the trek north. And, of course, we can always use the fresh meat. That is unless you want me to come to help you with your trading, Kent?"

"Your help would be welcome but I think I can do it on my own. I watched you when you were bartering in the villages we stopped at on the way here so I know how to do it. And if I get in trouble, I'll have Cru to help me."

Since they had loaded their packs the night before, they were ready to leave the next morning as soon as they had eaten. Yani called to Wolf as she left the house. But rather than joining her, he remained in his place by the fire. "What's wrong, Wolf? Don't you want to go for a short trip to Tam's village?"

She knelt by him and scratched behind his ears. He looked up at her and whined. As she talked softly to him, he licked her hands. "You know I'll be gone overnight. Are you sure you don't want to go too?" He whined again and then laid his head down and closed his eyes.

"Let me get a bowl of water and some meat for him," said Etta. "He should be alright since we are only going to be gone one night. And Deet will probably be back by dark."

"Thank you," replied Yani.

Kent, Cru and Black appeared at the door as Etta was returning from the stream with a bowl of water for Wolf.

"Wolf is not going with us. He seems really tired this morning. I'm making sure he will have water and food until we get back. And Deet should be back before night. So Wolf won't be alone very long," said Yani.

"I hope he's alright," said Cru.

"I think he is just tired," said Yani as she joined them in front of the house.

As they left the village, Black stopped and barked. Then running back to Yani's house barked again. "Come on, Black. We need to get moving if we're going to get to Tam's village in time for Kent to trade," said Cru.

But Black just whined and stayed where he was. They watched him a few moments puzzled. He barked once more and then tried to push the door open to enter the house.

"I think he wants to stay with Wolf," said Etta. "Is that what you want Black?" She walked back and flipped the leather door up so it caught on the roof. As soon as the door was opened, Black walked in and laid down beside Wolf.

"Well, I guess that settles it. Black wants to keep Wolf company," laughed Yani. "Did you put out enough for both of them?"

"They will have plenty for today and Deet will give them more when he comes back. And besides, they can always walk to the stream for water and if they get too hungry, Black is a good hunter," said Etta.

As they walked along the well-worn trail, Yani reminisced about the time she and the Knapper made this journey. "He was very weak but wanted to go. He had thought it would only take us half a day but because he had to stop and rest so often it was after dark when we finally got there. That is when I knew he would never be able to make the journey back to our beach on the North Sea. It was on this trip that I thought of making the traveling pack." Yani laughed remembering the trouble she had getting Wolf to pull it. "Deet helped me make the harness but I made the traveling pack by myself. Making it was the easy part. The hard part was getting Wolf to pull it. Hava finally came up with the solution. Wolf is male so of course he could be bribed with food."

"That's not very nice, Yani," said Cru

"That may be, but it's true. Can't I get you to do almost anything for something good to eat?" Cru looked up at her ready to argue until he saw the big smile on her face.

"Anyway, Hava brought me several scraps of meat. I let Wolf smell the meat then I backed away. I held out a piece of meat and as soon as he came to me, I gave him that scrap. It wasn't long before he was following me all around the village."

They walked along in silence for a while then Yani said, "It was a very good thing that I did train Wolf to pull the traveling pack. As it was Knut had to ride in it much of the way back north."

It was early afternoon when they arrived at Tam's village. As they entered the common area in the center of the village Yani heard someone call her name. Turning to the sound she saw an old woman with dark skin walking toward her. "Yani, I thought you would never come. But here you are at last."

"Hava? Is it you?" asked Yani as she closed the distance between them. When they met the two women hugged. Holding each other at arm's length they looked at each other smiling.

Hava took Yani by the hand and said, "Come, let's go let Tam know you're here. Then I want you to tell me everything that has happened to you since I last saw you."

"Everything?" asked Yani. "I'm afraid we don't have enough time for that."

"Well, at least the most important things," replied Hava.

When the visitors had let Tam know they were had arrived, Hava and Yani found a quiet spot in the shade to begin catching up. Tam took Kent to meet the men of the village who might want to barter for blades. Cru tagged along with Kent. Etta finding herself at loose ends, settled in the shade near enough to Hava and Yani to hear them but not to disturb them. Listening to the two friends reminisce, the musical quality of Hava's voice soon lulled Etta to sleep.

As Yani finished the tale of her years since seeing Hava she said, "So you see Hava, I have had a long and exciting life. So now I want to hear from you."

Etta woke up in time to hear Hava begin to tell Yani of the sickness that all but wiped out Gyla's village. "Yani, it was terrible. It happened so fast. A hunter from south of the mountains stumbled into the village one afternoon. He was so sick he couldn't even tell us his name or where he was from. Gyla took him into her house to nurse him but not before half the village had gathered to see if anyone recognized him. By the next day he was burning with fever and by that evening he was dead. We buried him in the manner I remember from my life in the south. We thought that would be the last of it but a few days later our people started to get sick. Soon people started to die. I got it but somehow, I survived. Everyone else in the village died. Even Gyla. One of the hunters from Tank's village started to come into the village early in the sickness. Luckily, Gyla saw him before he came close enough to catch the sickness. She told him to go home and tell everyone in his village to stay away. That is why this village survived. I was the only one from my village who lived.

They sat quietly for a few moments. Then Hava continued. "The hunter told Tank what was happening here and their medicine woman came to help Gyla. They both did their best, but not only could they not save the people, but they couldn't even save themselves.

"I remember knowing I had caught the sickness and thinking I would die like everyone else. I went into my house and laid down on my sleeping bench. The fever soon took over and I had all kinds of bad dreams. I don't know how long it lasted but the next thing I knew Deet had his arm around me lifting me off the bed. He was holding a bowl of water to my lips trying to get me to drink. He took care of me until I was strong enough to walk. Once I could make the trip he took me to Tank's village. I've been here ever since."

"That's awful. Do you know what the sickness was?" asked Yani.

"I remember hearing of a similar sickness when I was a child but it was in a village far from the one I grew up in, so I'm not sure if it was the same one."

As the day was ending, Tam joined the women. "I have come to let you know my lifemate would like you to join us for the evening meal. She has fixed something special in your honor, Yani. And, of course, you are invited, too, Hava."

"Thank you, Tam, I would love to join you. Yani and I have talked all afternoon but still have much to tell each other. And how did you spend your day? Did you help Kent with his trading?"

Laughing Tam said, "Actually, I did some trading of my own. I'm now the proud owner of three blades made by one of the newest knappers in the area. He drove a hard bargain but look at what I got in exchange for two rare pink feathers and a shiny black rock." Tam held out three of Cru's blades for them to see.

"I hope what you traded wasn't of great value," said Yani. "Cru is learning fast but I'm afraid that his blades aren't going to be ones you would want to hunt with."

"I disagree," objected Tam, "I think they are priceless. If you could have seen the pride in that boy as he offered me his blades. How could I not have made the deal? He will be a skilled knapper one day and I can say I made the first deal with him.”

“That’s very kind of you, Tam. I see the promise in him also and I’m sure what you have done today will do more to encourage him than anything I could say,” replied Yani.

“Well, whenever you’re ready Hava can show you the way to my house.”

As Tam walked away Yani said to Etta, “Will you go see if you can find a couple good blades in my pack that we can take as a gift to Tam. I don’t want him to feel cheated by the boy.”

“Wait, Etta,” said Hava. “Yani, I wish you wouldn’t. If Cru finds out he will think his blades are not worthy of the bargain he made. I know the items that Tam traded. Yes, they are unusual but not valuable. The feathers are from a bird that is common in the south. It is an odd-looking bird with long legs and a long neck. It eats a small sea creature that turns its feathers pink. I had dozens of those feathers as a child. And Tam found that rock in the stream above the village. If you walk up that way you will find more. It sounds like Cru is satisfied with his trade and I can tell you that Tam is too. Let it stand.”

“You are right, Hava. I wasn’t thinking.”

# Chapter Seven

Yani and her group left early the next day for their return trip to Gyla's village. They had had a good visit with Tam and his family but Yani was anxious to get back and check on Wolf. He had been so weak when they left him. The two young medicine women walked a ways with them as they left. "Yani, we would like to come and visit with you one day soon," said Kal. "I'm sure there is much you can teach us."

"I would like that very much," answered Yani. "And I have some herbs that are not found here that I would like to give you. I must be getting old and forgetful because I should have brought them with me. Oh, well, that's just another reason for you to come see me."

After a while, the young medicine women bid them goodbye and returned to the village. When the visitors were alone, Cru moved over so he was by Etta's side. They had not gone far when Cru said to her, "Do you want to see what I traded three of my blades for?"

Looking down at the boy she said in mock surprise, "You traded some of your blades? That means you are a real knapper and a real trader. How wonderful. Who did you trade with?"

"Well, I'm not sure I'm a real trader but I guess I am starting to be a knapper. But it was good practice for when I become a real knapper," he replied.

"No, Cru, if you made blades that are good enough that someone wanted them then you are a real knapper. Maybe not a really, really good one but a knapper, nonetheless. So, what did you trade for?"

As they walked Cru rummaged in his pouch and finally pulled out two large pink feathers. He handed them to Etta to examine. "Cru, those are lovely. You must take good care of them since they are so unusual. Who did you say you traded with?"

"It was Tam. And he also gave me this." Digging around in his pouch he came up with a shiny round black stone that had been shaped by the water as it rolled along the bottom of the stream. "I gave him my three best blades and he gave me these. Do you think I made a fair trade?"

"Cru, you did very good. I'm proud of you. When we get back to the Valley, I can see you becoming our knapper," said Etta.

Cru walked along silently for a while then he said, "Yani isn't going to go back with us, is she?"

Sighing, Etta replied, "I don't think so. She hasn't exactly said so but I think she's planning to stay here. I'm not sure she could make the trip. Have you noticed that she is walking slower than usual? And she spends a lot of time just sitting looking at the mountains."

"But if she stays here does that mean Deet is going to leave her? And if he doesn't come with us, how will we get home. Kent can't do it because he's an outlaw. I know they don't mind here but on the other side of the Steppes, they do. Doesn't this mean I won't ever see my mother and father and Dan again." As he finished Cru teared up.

"Cru, I will get us home. I promise you that. If I can't do it this winter, I will do it next spring. I have been asking Deet questions about the trail home and he also knows it will be just you and I returning to the Valley. But for now, let's not think about it. Let's talk about what all we learned from getting to know the people in Tam's village."

Cru reached out and took Etta's hand. "I'm glad you're my friend."

Tousling the boy's hair Etta answered, "And I'm awfully glad you're my friend."

They had crossed the stream and were nearing the village when Etta saw Deet walking toward them. There was something in his carriage that told Etta that all was not well. When Yani saw him, she called out, "Hello, Deet. What I nice surprise that you've come to meet us. Did you have a successful hunt?"

Deet just waved at them and kept walking until he was by Yani's side. Placing his hands on her shoulders he stopped her. Looking down at her he said, "Yani, my little butterfly, I have some very sad news. We have lost a good and faithful friend."

"What do you mean?" she asked. "Everyone is here with us. Who do you…"?

Tears filled Yani's eyes as she realized who Deet meant. "Oh, Deet, not Wolf."

"I'm sorry Yani. When I got back last night he was not doing well, I offered him water and some of the fresh venison from my kill yesterday but he just looked up at me and whined. I made him as comfortable as I could. I was hoping he was just very tired but when morning came, he was gone. Black had stayed by his side. It looks like he just went quietly in his sleep." When Deet finished he pulled Yani into his arms and held her as she cried.

"Deet, why did I leave him? If I had thought he was so sick I never would have," Yani said through her tears.

"Yani, he wanted it this way. I have noticed he has been getting weaker. And you must remember, Wolf has lived an awfully long time. Much longer than a wolf usually does. Now let's go home and we can send him to the Otherside in the proper way."

With his arm over her shoulder Deet lead Yani back toward the village. The others followed at a distance giving them some privacy. They could hear their voices as they talked quietly back and forth but couldn't make out what they were saying..

The high spirits they had all started out with that morning had been replaced with sadness. Black came to greet Cru as they entered the village but he was not his usual rambunctious self. Kneeling and burying his face in Black's fur, Cru whispered, "You are a good boy, Black. You were here to take care of Wolf."

As the others continued to the house where Wolf's body rested, Cru stayed outside with Black. He didn't want to add his tears to those that he knew Yani would be crying. When Kent emerged from the house carrying Wolf, Cru left Black's side and joined him. Soon the others followed. They carried Wolf to the spot at the edge of the forest where he often would sleep in the afternoon. The sun would filter through the trees and warm his old bones as he lay there. Clearing a patch big enough to hold Wolf, Etta took a hoe blade and scrapped a shallow hole big enough for Wolf to fit in. When it was deep enough Yani scattered some fragrant herbs in the bottom. That done, she moved back to stand beside Deet as Kent laid Wolf on the sweet-scented bed. Etta and Cru then covered his body with the dirt that Etta had dug to make the grave. Once they had Wolf covered Etta, Kent and Cru went to the stream and began carrying rocks to cover the grave. It was getting dark when they were satisfied that there were enough rocks to keep wild animals from digging up Wolf's remains.

After they had all said their goodbyes to their old friend they returned to the house. When they reached the door, Kent bid them goodnight and went off to the house he had taken as his own. They entered the house and Etta said, "Yani, you go rest. I'll fix something for us to eat."

"Thank you, Etta. I think I'll just go to sleep. I'm not very hungry. But the rest of you need to eat." With that, Yani crawled on to her sleeping bench and rolled up in her sleeping cloak.

Etta went about preparing something for them to eat. Cru picked up the cooking pot and headed to the stream for water without being told to. By the time he was back Etta had found the acorn meal and some pieces of the dried fish they had brought with them from the Valley. She thought maybe a taste of home would ease their sadness.

When the porridge was done, she ladled some into bowls and handed one to each of them. Deet ate a few bites then saying he wasn't hungry he joined Yani on the sleeping bench. Etta nudged Cru and with a flick of her head let Cru know they should go outside to eat. Taking their bowls, they left the house and settled down near the firepit. As they ate a full moon appeared over the mountains.

"It's alright to cry if you want to, Cru. We're all going to miss Wolf. I may cry a little bit myself," said Etta with a sniff. As they sat there watching the moon, tears rolled down their cheeks. It was late when the two young people finally entered the house.

# Chapter Eight

"Cru!" called Deet. "Where are you?"

"I'm over here by the stream," came the answer.

"Do you want to go hunting with me?"

"Yes! I'm coming. Don't leave without me," Cru yelled as he gathered up his basket and ran toward the village.

When he reached Deet he asked, "Where are we going? What are we going to hunt for?"

"So many questions!" said Deet with a chuckle. "First off we're going to head up the trail toward the mountain. There's a watering hole on the stream up there where lots of animals come to drink. As to what we're going to hunt, that depends on what is thirsty today. I'm hoping to get a deer but if none show we'll see what we can get. Go tell Yani you're going with me."

Cru started into the house where Yani was. Deet stopped him and said, "By the way Cru do you have a spear with one of your blades on it?"

"Yes," answered Cru hesitantly.

"You better bring it. Now is a good time to see how well you've learned to make blades."

Cru ducked under the leather door covering. Deet could hear him explaining to Yani that he was going hunting with Deet. He could hear the pride in Cru's voice when he told her that Deet was going to use a spear with his own point on it.

They kept up a steady walking pace as they climbed the gentle rise of the trail leading to the mountains. When they reached the game trail that led to the watering hole Deet told Cru that from here on they needed to be silent. As they moved along the narrow trail they avoided stepping on twigs. The noise of a breaking twig could be heard by any game that might be in the area. As they moved through the forest they walked with an uneven pace. A step or two then a pause. Only man walked at a steady even pace.

When they reached the watering hole Deet pointed to a spot behind a small shrub. He motioned for Cru to hunker down there to wait and watch. As he settled in place Cru offered his spear to Deet. But Deet shook his head. Whispering he said, "You will use that spear. It's time you make your first kill."

"But I've already killed fish and squirrels," whispered Cru.

"They don't count. Today you're going to kill your first deer."

Deet smiled at the look of shock on Cru's face. It was unusual for a boy this young to kill his first deer but Deet suspected that Cru was ready. And even if he wasn't it was time to get him ready. He would need this skill when he and Etta made the trek back to the Valley. Etta and Cru weren't much more than children but it was clear that when the time came, they would be making the journey alone.

Cru had to use all his patience to sit quietly as they waited. He knew any movement could alert a deer that might be coming to drink. As he waited, he wet his finger and tested the wind. There wasn't much of a breeze but what there was blew into his face. He knew this was good because the wind would blow their scent away. That is if Deet had guessed right and the deer would be coming down the trail in front of them and not come along from behind them. Of course, Cru knew Deet would have watched this watering hole off and on since they had arrived here in the south. He would know the pattern of the animals' movements.

When Cru was almost to the end of his ability to sit quietly, Deet touched his arm and pointed. Cru looked where Deet was pointing he saw a young buck picking his way down the trail toward the water. Deet motioned for Cru to stand. When the buck reached the water, he lowered his head to drink. Deet had picked the perfect spot for them to wait. The deer was in a position for a kill. His head was down so he could not easily see them. Most important he was standing so that they had a clear shot to hit him in the heart if they were lucky. If they missed the heart, they would at least hit one of his vital organs.

Deet whispered, "Now." Cru threw his spear. A split second later Deet also threw. When Cru's spear hit the buck, it buried deep into the deer's side. An instant later Deet's spear also hit the mark. The deer's head jerked up. He stumbled for a few steps then bolted off into the forest. Calling to Cru to follow, Deet began to go after the buck. Using the trail of blood to lead them, they were able to track the injured animal through the woods.

"It is important that we find the deer so we can free his spirit and offer thanks. The gods will be angry if we have killed and don't use the meat. This is very important. Do you understand?" asked Deet.

"Yes," answered Cru. "Etta taught me this when we caught the trout in the stream. But I knew it from what I have heard the hunters back in the Valley say."

They tracked the deer for most of the day. "He's much stronger than I would have thought," said Deet. "To have come this far with two spears in his side. And they went deep or they would have fallen out of the wounds by now. But we haven't found them so they're still in him."

The light was fading when they finally found the deer. His front legs had buckled and he was resting on his chest. When he heard the hunters coming, he tried to rise but he didn't have the strength. He had lost too much blood. Slowly approaching, Deet said to Cru, "Here is my knife. Now you must go to the deer and end his life. Be sure to say the thank you first, then with a swift cut slit his throat. And Cru, be careful of his antlers. He may still have some fight left in him."

Nodding, Cru took the knife and cautiously approached the deer. Talking calmly and quietly, Cru began the ritual of thanks. He had just finished when he was close enough to touch the deer. With one hand he quickly grabbed the antlers and bent the deer's head back. With the other hand he ran the knife firmly across the deer's throat. As he watched, the life went out of the deer's eyes. Lowering its head to the ground, Cru pulled Deet's spear from the deer's side. Turning to Deet he handed him the spear. Then he turned back and retrieved his spear.

Clapping Cru on the shoulder, Deet said, "Well Cru, you're now a hunter. How do you feel about that?"

"I'm not sure. I'm proud to know that I can provide meat for my family, but sad that I have to kill such a beautiful creature to do it. Is that wrong?"

Turning the boy so he could look him in the eye, Deet said, "No Cru, that is not wrong. That's the right way to feel. That's why we always thank the animal for his life and release his spirit as quickly and painlessly as possible. You did well. Now let's get this deer back to the village before dark."

When they had bled and gutted the deer, Deet tied its feet together and ran the spear shafts through the legs. Cru lifted his end of the spears and rested it on his shoulder. Deet rested his end on his hip so it was nearly level with Cru's end and they started back down the mountain.

It was full dark when they finally neared the village. They met Etta and Kent who had started out the trail to look for the hunters. When Etta saw them, she called out, "Deet, Cru, we were getting worried. Are you alright?"

"Are we alright, oh mighty hunter Cru?" asked Deet.

"I'm alright. Just really tired. Could one of you take my end?" said Cru as he staggered forward. Kent ran up to him and took the end of spear the deer was hanging from him. As soon as he relieved Cru of his burden, the boy dropped down on to the ground. "Can I just rest a few minutes, please?" he asked.

Laughing, Etta scooped him up and throwing him over her shoulder said, "No you can't. We need to get home so we can help Deet butcher his deer. And if he'll let me have it, I want to get a nice cut of the deer on the fire to slow cook for breakfast."

Deet shook his head and told Etta, "I'm afraid I can't give you a cut of this deer."

"Oh," said Etta. "Were you going to give it to Tam or Hava as a gift? Or maybe someone else?"

"No, I can't give this deer to anyone because it's not my kill. And I think you should show more respect to the hunter who did kill it. Do you think it right to carry a hunter of deer over your shoulder like a tired puppy?" he replied.

Giggling, Cru said, "It's alright if she treats me like a puppy right now. I'm so tired I don't care. And as long as I get the first cut off the chunk of meat you want to cook, you can have any that you want."

"Cru, I am so proud of you!" said Etta. "I can't wait for Yani to hear."

"And I used one of my own blades," said Cru.

"Then you are now a knapper and a trader as well as a hunter. I am so proud of you, Cru."

"I just wish I could tell Father and Mother and Dan," said Cru.

# Chapter Nine

Cru woke to the delightful aroma of roasting meat. He lay there on his sleeping bench of a while remembering the events of the day before. He had made his first real kill making him a hunter. And best of all he had made the kill with one of his own blades. Kent had said he was a real trader and a real knapper. Deet said he was a real hunter. So did that mean he was old enough that he and Etta could make the journey home on their own. He had figured out that it would just be the two of them. Yani had said she wasn't going and when he watched her these days, he could see that she was no longer strong enough to go. And Deet would never leave Yani. Kent had made a home for himself here and had even started looking for a possible life mate among the young women in Tam's village. That meant if he were going to get home it would be just he and Etta.

Finally, the smell of the cooking meat was more than he could stand. His stomach was rumbling, reminding him that he had eaten little the day before. Crawling out of bed he walked out to the firepit where the rest of the group were working on the meat from his deer. Squatting down beside Yani, he asked, "Is that meat ready to eat?"

"If you like it on the rare side, it is," she answered.

"To be honest, I'm hungry enough to eat it raw," he replied.

"Then I would say it's done enough," Yani gingerly took the spit of meat from the fire and cut a generous portion from it which she handed it to Cru. He blew on it to cool it enough he wouldn't burn his mouth. As soon as he felt he could safely eat it he took a large bite.

"So how is it?" asked Etta. "Does the fact you killed it make it taste better?"

"I'm not sure if that's it, or that I'm starving, but it tastes mighty good," he said.

Later in that moon as Etta was looking for trout in the stream, she saw the two medicine women from Tam's village walking down the trail toward the village. Calling out to them she climbed out of the steam and went to meet them.

"Welcome," Etta called out. "Yani was wondering when you two were going to show up."

"We decided this would be a perfect day for a visit since it is the right time to dig sunflower roots for drying," said Kal.

"And we happened to know there's a large patch of them a short way back the trail toward the Steppes," added Min.

"We thought Yani would like to go with us to dig some," said Kal.

"Let's go ask her," said Etta. Chatting as they walked, the three women made their way to Yani's house.

When they entered, Yani was sitting by the firepit watching the small blaze that burned there. "Yani," said Etta as they entered. "Look, we have company."

Looking up Yani smiled weakly. "Kal and Min, welcome. Come sit down and rest. Are you hungry?"

"We'll be glad of the rest but we're not hungry. At least I'm not. Are you, Min?"

"No, I'm fine."

"Yani, they have come to collect sunflower root and want to know if you would like to join them. They tell me there is a big patch a short way down the trail toward the Steppes," said Etta.

"Yes, I remember that patch of sunflowers. Gyla and I gathered there the summer she taught me about herbs. But I'm not sure I'm up to the walk. Maybe Etta would like to go with you."

As the three women walked along the trail, Kal asked, "Is Yani not well?"

"She is just getting old and tired," said Etta. "I worry about her."

"Is she going to be able to make the trip back to your home?" asked Min.

"No, I don't think she will. I think she is planning on staying here," replied Etta.

"Then are you all going to stay?" asked Kal.

"My plan is to take Cru and go home," said Etta.

"Just the two of you?" asked Kal. "Aren't you afraid to go alone?"

"Yes," replied Etta, "but that is the only way Cru and I will get home."

When they reached the patch of sunflowers, they began to dig out the plump roots. It didn't take long for each of them to have filled the baskets they brought to hold them. When they had collected all they needed, they carried the baskets to the stream that ran along the side of the trail. Kneeling at the water's edge, they began washing the roots. As they worked, they chatted as young women do.

"So, Etta, what can you tell us about Kent. Does he have a lifemate waiting for him on the other side of the Steppes?" asked Kal.

"No, he doesn't," replied Etta.

"I wonder why?" asked Min. "He's very handsome and also a knapper. I would think that he would have found a mate by now."

"I don't think he has found the right one," said Etta.

"Maybe he'll find one here," giggled Min.

"That would be very nice," said Etta. "But I think if we have these roots clean enough, we should head back. I don't like to leave Yani alone for too long."

As they returned to the village, Min and Kal peppered Etta with questions about Kent. Etta was careful to avoid giving a real answer to them. If Kent wanted these young women to know his story he would tell them himself.

When they arrived back at the village, Etta spread her sunflower roots to dry in the sun. As she was working on this, the two visitors went into the house to visit with Yani.

When Etta entered the house Kal was showing Yani the herbs they had brought to give her. "I am fairly sure that these plants don't grow in your Valley since I have never seen them on the other side of the Steppe. We brought several bags of each for you to take back with you when you go north."

Picking each bag up and inspecting it Yani finally said, "I thank you but it is Etta you should be giving these to. I have decided to stay here. She is the one who will be going back to the Valley." Handing the bags to Etta she said, "Why don't you put these in your medicine pouch?"

"Maybe Kal should tell me what they are and the uses before I put them away," suggested Etta.

"Of course," said Yani. "Here look at this one and then Kal can tell you about it."

As the day waned Kal and Min made sure Etta knew what needed to be known about the herbs they had brought. When she was confident, she knew about them, Etta brought her medicine pouch and began digging through it. "I'm sure there are some I have that don't grow here. Yani; what should I give them?"

When Deet and Cru came in it was too late in the day for the women to start back to their village. They helped Etta fix food for the evening meal and when it was ready Etta said to Cru, "Why don't you go see if Kent would like to join us for supper."

Cru jumped up and headed out the door to go get Kent. As he did, he noticed the bright color on Min cheeks.

## Chapter Ten

Several days later, Cru saw Etta heading for the forest trail with a couple of large baskets. "Etta, where are you going?" he called.

"I'm going up the trail to that clearing where the big white oak tree is. I think the acorns have started to fall. We're running low on acorn meal so I wanted to get some before the squirrels beat me to them."

"Can I come too?" he asked. "I'm good at picking up acorns. I always used to help Mother every fall."

"I never turn down help," replied Etta. "Come on."

As they walked along the trail, Cru kicked at the dry leaves that had fallen from the oak and maple trees that lined the path. "We're not going home this winter, are we, Etta?" asked the boy.

"No, I don't think we are," she replied.

"Are we ever going home?" he asked quietly.

"Cru, I promise you this – I will take you home. It may not happen until next spring but we are going home."

'But, Etta, if Yani and Deet and Kent all plan on staying here how can we go home. You don't think we can make that trip alone do you?"

"Cru, look at me," she said taking him by his shoulders. When he looked up at her, she said, "We are going home even if it's just the two of us. I've been thinking about it a lot. I think I have figured out a way."

"But, Etta, how? It's an awfully long way and I'm afraid we will get lost."

"I've been talking to Deet. When I get it all figured out, I'll explain it to you. But now we need to get everything ready. Making acorn meal is step one. We'll have to eat on the journey. Since we won't be doing a lot of trading, we'll need to take our own food. So, let's go get those acorns collected."

That afternoon, Etta and Cru returned to the village with two baskets loaded with acorns. As soon as they had eaten a quick lunch, they began the process of cracking the acorns and removing their outer shell. They had set up near the firepit so they could throw the shells into the pit as they worked. The nut meat they placed in a basket that had a loose enough weave to allow water to flow through but tight enough that the nut meat would stay in it. When they had the basket full Etta carried it to the stream. She placed the basket in the water where it was deep enough that the acorns were completely covered. As the water flowed through the basket it would leach the bitterness out of the acorns. They would need to be in the stream for a couple of days to remove all the tannin from them. Once they had done that, the acorns would need to be dried before being ground into meal. Checking to see that the basket was tied securely, Etta turned to Cru and said, "One basket done. Let's get back and finish the other. I was not expecting to get this done today but with your help it looks like we will."

Cru lagged behind a bit as they returned to the firepit. He looked longingly toward where Kent was working. As he walked, he mumbled to himself, "I wish I were making blades but I guess if I'm going to get home I have to crack stupid acorns."

They had the last of the acorns cracked and in to soak as the light faded. As they gathered for the evening meal, Yani commented on the acorn harvest. "It looks like you have gathered enough to keep us in meal for this winter and then some. I'm not sure we'll need all that."

"It's always better to have more than we need," replied Etta. "You never know what's going to happen. Tomorrow I'm going to look around and see if maybe there's a grindstone here in the village. Maybe one got left when the villagers went to live at Tam's village."

"That sounds like a promising idea," said Yani. "We will need one. If you don't find one, we will have to make one. It can be done but is hard work. Let hope someone forgot to take one."

# Chapter Eleven

As winter set in, Etta began to make her plans for the trip north. While they sat around the fire in the evening, she used the scraps of deer skin left over from making their new moccasins to make small pouches. Her plan as to put some of the herbs she and Yani had dried into them so she would have them to offer in exchange for a place to sleep on the trip north. She was thinking that if no one in the village offered them shelter, the village medicine woman would in exchange of the herbs.

Etta had been encouraging Cru to make flakes from the flint found in the stream. He was getting better at making blades and if he had the flakes he could continue to make blades as they moved north. His blades were not the fine ones that Yani made but he could make serviceable knives. That was another thing to use in exchange for food and shelter. Of course, she was hoping that most villages would welcome them as guests.

As Etta made her plans, Yani watched. She was hoping Etta would confide in her soon so she could help her with her preparation. It was clear that Etta was planning to return to the Valley. Finally, one evening as Etta was cutting a deer hide to make a new vest for Cru, Yani asked, "When are you planning on leaving?"

Looking startled, Etta said, "Leaving for where?"

"Etta, I can see what you're planning. I've watched your preparations most of the winter. The extra acorn meal. The flint flakes that you are encouraging Cru to make. The new moccasins for both of you. Now the new vest for Cru. So, I ask, when are you planning on leaving?"

Sighing, Etta replied, "I was thinking of leaving in the early spring. The grass will not be high on the Steppes yet so I won't miss the markers. Also, the springs will be flowing so water won't be a problem. Once we get across the Steppes I think we will be all right. The Steppes is the part that has been worrying me. I'm not sure I can find the way back across them on my own. But after that I had decided if I asked directions at each village to the next village, we could make our way home."

"That's sound planning. I'll hate to see you go but I know you must. We did promise to get Cru back home to his family. Now, if you take a piece of that deer hide and give it to Deet, I am sure he can draw you a map that will help you find your way. In the meantime, what can I do to help you prepare?"

Rising from her place by the fire, Etta walked over to Yani. Sitting on the sleeping bench beside her she wrapped her arms around Yani and said, "Thank you. I'll miss you. I don't really want to leave you but we did promise to take Cru back home. I have to do this."

"I know you do," replied Yani. "You have been a wonderful daughter and I'll be lonely without you. But you're right. Cru needs to go home."

As the leaves began to bud, Etta and Cru loaded their packs for the journey before them. Yani checked and double checked to make sure Etta had all the things she might need. For the past moon Deet had spent time with Cru teaching him as much as he could about hunting and making snares. He made sure that Cru had a good sturdy spear for protection.

On the morning they planned to leave, Cru went to tell the goats goodbye. Etta had decided she didn't want the added responsibility of two goats. Since they were not carrying trade goods except the few things they planned to use for gifts, the goats were staying with Yani. When he returned from the goat pen, Yani, and Kent were waiting to tell them goodbye. He gave each of his friends a big hug. "I'll miss you," he said through tears. "And thank you for all you have taught me. Goodbye." He shouldered his pack and said , "Come on, Black, let's get going."

Etta watched as he started up the trail. She knew he would need a few moments to cry before she and Deet caught up to him. Hugging Yani, she said, "I'll never forget you. And I'll miss you terribly. Who knows, maybe one day I'll come back."

"Go now before I decide I can't let you go," Yani said hugging her tighter. Then she broke away and entered the house.

After a quick goodbye to Kent, Etta said, "Well, Deet we better be on our way before we lose Cru on the Steppes. He may just keep walking when he gets there and go to the wrong starting point."

It was getting dark when they reached the cave. Cru set to work gathering firewood and soon they had a cozy fire going. As Etta cooked some acorn porridge, Deet asked to see the map he had made her. When she handed it to him, he looked at it for a long time. Then he said, "Let's go over this one more time. I want to make sure you know the way."

"Deet, please," Etta said. "Let's just visit tonight. I have been over that so many times I can tell you the way with my eyes closed. And to be sure I'll ask at each village."

Folding the map and handing it back to Etta, he said, "You're right. It's just that I wish I were going all the way with you. But I…"

"Deet, I know. You can't leave Yani. And I wouldn't want you to. Cru and I will do fine, won't we Cru."

"I'll take good care of her. And we have Black to protect us, too," said Cru.

"Now let's enjoy are last time together," said Etta.

The sun was painting the grasses of the Steppes a rosy pink when they stepped out of the forest. They looked out across the wide expanse, then turned and walked toward the rising sun. The pink was beginning to fade from the grass when Deet stopped them. "Here is the start of the path north. If you look you can see the first of the marker stones. Follow them the same way we followed the ones coming. Stay alert and you'll do fine."

With that he quickly hugged them both, then turning he started back to where the trail entered the forest. Etta and Cru watched until he disappeared from sight.

Once he disappeared into the trees, Etta looked down at the boy and said, "Come on, Cru, let's go home."

# About the Author

Cherie Coon grew up in the small southeastern Ohio village of Laurelville. After graduating from Laurelville High School (known as Toad Run Academy in the days when her grandmother attended) she went on to study at THE Ohio State University. While there she received a degree in Elementary Education. After graduation she taught in Lake City, Florida before returning to Ohio. She continued teaching in the Circleville area until her first husband uprooted the family to follow a career in the military. For the next twenty years her life was one of a modern-day camp follower. With each change of station, Cherie found herself in a different job. Sometimes it was in education but often it was whatever turned up. From 1988 to 1994 she lived in Berlin, Germany where she taught the children of our military at Thomas A. Roberts Elementary School. During her time in Berlin she experienced the fall of the Berlin Wall, became an active member of the spinning and weaving group at the Museumsdorf Duppel (a living museum in the American Sector), and traveled to the USSR as the communist government was crumbling.

When she left Berlin it was as a single woman. She transferred to Ansbach, Germany where she lived for the next sixteen years. During this time she continued her career with the Department of Defense Dependent Schools teaching the children of our military men and women stationed there. As she was nearing retirement she met and married her current husband, David. When she retired they first moved to southern California. After three years in the LA sprawl, they moved north to the small Oregon town of Grants Pass.

Cherie has been a writer of sorts all her life. Her first stories were the ones she created as a small child with her imaginary friends, Orangie and Diann. She has dabbled in poetry, travel journals, and short stories. Until she retired though she never seriously took up the pen. In 2010 while talking to a friend who had just published her first book, she decided to dig out the novel she had started while living in Ansbach. She likes to say her first book took twenty years to write, after that not quite so long. She has authored a three-book series *The Saga of Yani* which includes *Yani and the Knapper – The Journey, Yani and the Seapeople – Taken , Yani and Etta- A New Beginning.* Now her new series Etta's Story will continue the adventures with Yani's adopted daughter, Etta.

Now Book Clubs and School Classes can schedule a

# Chat with the Author
# Zoom Meeting

## To schedule a meeting email

sagaofyani@yahoo.com